Prologue

21 years ago

Nikki pulled into the narrow driveway of her old family home. Usually, the salty and cool Seattle air would fill her with feelings of euphoria. That Sunday afternoon was totally different.

She sighed and switched off the ignition, staring into the abyss before her.

"I'm sorry, Miss Murphy, but I'm afraid you won't be able to have children."

"What do you mean I can't have children? How is that possible? It can't be that serious."

"Polycystic ovarian syndrome often has that effect. I'm really sorry, but maybe you and your husband can consider alternative ways of making a family, but I'm afraid you won't be able to have one of your own."

"It's either ours or it's not happening."

Josh's words had rung loud and clear, and tears dotted

the corners of Nikki's eyes. She hadn't told her parents the news yet, but she didn't anticipate any sympathy from them. They hadn't been too pleased that she'd run off and married Josh without their knowledge.

Her father was all about news, and as a respected and reputable journalist, he would have wanted a story about his daughter—one that involved a beautiful beachfront wedding. He'd been furious with her since. He'd probably interpret her news as just punishment, which was why she hadn't told them.

She lifted her eyes to the rearview mirror and gasped at her appearance. Her mascara had muddied her eyes, making her look like a raccoon. She quickly reached for her makeup kit in her purse, knocking the contents onto the floor as she did.

She cursed under her breath as she leaned over and tried to gather the items. Her torso accidentally hit the horn, and the loud beep startled her.

"Okay, Nikki," she said as she inhaled deeply. "Get it together. Now isn't the time to fall apart."

She ruffled her dirty-blond hair, pinched her cheeks to get back some color, and smeared her favorite peach-colored lipstick onto her plump lips. "That should do it," she said as she looked at her reflection. "It's now or never."

She got out of the car and, with anchor legs, walked up the porch steps. Her hand was suspended in the air and ready to knock when she heard Trish scream.

"No!"

"You don't have a choice," her father shouted.

What on earth?

Nikki didn't bother knocking. Panic seized her in the chest, and she fumbled frantically in her purse for the house keys. She opened the door with shaky fingers and closed it gently behind her.

She treaded softly, almost expecting to get attacked by a ferocious animal. She was barely breathing and half expected to see a dish come hurling toward her.

"Mom, please," Trish cried. "I don't want to go."

Nikki poked her head around the corner of the living room just as three pairs of eyes turned to her.

Her father, upon seeing her, threw his hands in the air. "Great! Here comes the other disappointment."

Nikki wrinkled her brows. "What did I do?"

"What did you do? What did you do?" he muttered to himself in disbelief.

Nikki could see stress written all over his face as he glared at her. The last time she'd seen him like that was when he'd found out she and Josh had eloped.

"Mom, what's going on?" Nikki asked as she ventured closer to her mother and Trish, who shrank back.

"None of your business," her father barked. "Why don't you just go back to Arlington? That's where you live now, right?"

Nikki couldn't understand how she'd become the topic of conversation and the object of his wrath just by walking into the house. "Will someone please tell me what's going on?" Nikki blurted out.

"Ask her!" Her father pointed at a very embarrassed Trish.

Even though they'd been raised by the same parents in the same household, Nikki and Trish had never been close. They'd just never seen eye to eye and were not as close as sisters should be.

But the fear she saw in her little sister's eyes melted

3

away years of indifference. "Trish," she said softly, walking over to her. "What happened?

Their mother sat gently on the edge of the sofa, her hands placed in her lap, and a sorrowful look on her face like someone had died.

"Will someone please answer me?" Nikki pleaded as she looked from one to the other. None seemed willing to reply.

"Okay, since *Trish* doesn't want to say it, I will," her father said in a booming voice. His gray hair seemed even more pronounced like he had aged since the last time she'd seen him. "Your sister got herself pregnant! There! Are you happy? You both seem intent on destroying my reputation and sending me to an early grave," he spat dramatically.

Nikki gasped and turned to Trish, who stared a hole into the floor. Her long blond hair hung in front of her, hiding her face, but Nikki could still make out the glistening tears on her cheeks.

"Oh, Trish," she said softly.

"Don't coddle her!" her father snapped. "She should have known better. She was supposed to go to Seattle University and get her degree in journalism, not get knocked up by some loser. What will everyone think?"

"Oh, come on, Stew," her mother finally spoke up. "I don't see what this has to do with you."

"Are you kidding me?" he asked and walked back to stand in front of his wife. "See, this is the problem right here. You let them get away with too much. Not this time. I will not stand for this."

"I don't get it," Nikki said as her brows dipped. "If she is already pregnant..." The thoughts formed quickly in her mind as she realized what her father was demanding. "Dad, what's going on?"

"She's not having that child is what's happening," he barked.

"What?" Nikki replied. "What do you mean not having it? Do you really want her to get an abortion? Wouldn't that be a worse feature in a gossip column than her being pregnant at all?"

"I don't want an abortion," Trish said weakly.

"Well then, how are you going to support the child? Huh?" Stew asked coldly like he wasn't talking about a human being or talking to his daughter. "Is that good-for-nothing going to marry you? Where is he, by the way? Oh right! He walked out on you and this kid. You're only nineteen, and I certainly am not going to take that on. Not at my age. And neither is Sophia. So where does that leave you?"

"What are you going to do?" Nikki wanted to know as her heart started to race. She was torn, considering she couldn't have a child, and there she was, caught up in a conversation with her family over an unwanted child.

"He wants to send me to Arlington because he's embarrassed. And then I must give up the baby for adoption," Trish replied sadly.

"That's right," Stew murmured. "That's the only solution at this point."

"I have another idea." All eyes stared expectantly at Nikki. "What if I adopt the baby?"

A tense silence descended upon the room just then, and Nikki looked around, hoping they would agree. She couldn't have a child of her own, and her sister couldn't keep the baby. It was perfect, and she was hopeful again for the first time in months.

Josh was adamant he didn't want to adopt a child, but maybe he'd think differently if he knew the baby was Trish's and not a stranger.

"Are you insane?" Stew finally spoke.

"Dad, think about it," Nikki said excitedly. "That's one of the reasons I came today. I found out that I can't have children. I have this condition that prevents it, but this," she said, turning to Trish. "This is a chance for Josh and me to have the family we won't be able to have. It's a blessing."

"No," her mother whispered. "That can't happen."

"What?" Nikki asked in dismay. "Why? You already plan on putting the baby up for adoption. Why can't I adopt her or him?"

"Because what's the sense in that?" Stew asked and circled her like a vulture. "Why do you think we're sending her to Arlington? So that you can come back here with the child after?"

"Dad, I already live in Arlington. No one would know. If you're worried about your reputation, no one has to know my connection to you or Trish. Just please, do this for me. Trish," she said, turning to her sister. She took both of her hands in hers and squeezed them. "I know we haven't always been the best of sisters, but don't deny me this one thing. I've never asked you for anything."

Trish hung her head. "I can't do it, Nikki." She sniffled. "If I have to give up this baby, I don't want to know anything about her or him. How do you think I'd feel if you came over? I'd know it's my child."

"Then we won't come over. We'll stay over there. Away from everyone."

Trish shook her head. "I can't."

Nikki was heartbroken, and tears welled up in her

eyes. "Are you all serious? You'd rather give the baby to a stranger than to me? Even after you know I can't have a child. Trish! This is your baby. Please!" Nikki pleaded again as the tears ran down her face.

Trish looked away, and her mother hung her head.

"I'm afraid that's for the best, dear." Sophia sighed. "I'm sure you'll find another baby you and Josh can adopt..."

"This is unbelievable!" Nikki exclaimed. "Mom, I expected this sort of behavior from Dad, but not from you. And Trish! I'm your sister. How could you do this to me?"

"I'm not doing anything to you, Nikki," Trish fired back. "It's not my fault you can't have children, but I can't give you mine."

"No. You'd prefer to give it to a stranger," Nikki said as the pain washed across her. "Mom, talk to him. I know this isn't you."

That was Nikki's last-ditch effort to get someone to be sympathetic with her. They all remained silent. She was sorely disappointed, and the tears flowed from her freely. She wiped her hand across her face and sighed.

"You know what? It's fine," she said as she picked up her purse. "I am your blood, and you'd do this to me. I want nothing more to do with any of you."

She walked away, and none of them tried to stop her as she slammed the front door shut. Tears blinded her as she ran to the car and got in. She leaned her head against the steering wheel as grief overcame her again. She relived the moments when she discovered she couldn't have children, and she lost track of time until her phone rang.

She slowly turned her head and saw that it was Josh. She hit the answer button.

"Hi," she said weakly.

"Hey. When are you getting back?" he asked.

"I'm on my way," Nikki replied as she turned the key in the ignition.

"Okay," he replied as he hung up.

Nikki dried her eyes and clenched her jaw as she stared with disdain at the home she had once loved. She put the car in reverse and backed out of the driveway, and as the car glided onto the empty street that was once so familiar to her, she looked one last time at the house she was sure she'd never see again.

Chapter One

The smell of fresh, roasted coffee filled the air, reminding Nikki she needed to take a break.

She'd been working on stories all morning, coming up with fresh approaches to a column her father had established many years ago.

She rubbed her eyes and walked to the kitchen, anxiously looking forward to the smooth, dark liquid.

The phone rang just as she was pouring the coffee, startling her and causing her to spill some onto the counter.

"Sheesh!" she exclaimed and tapped her earbuds. "Veronica, this had better be good."

Veronica, her editor, giggled. "Would I call you otherwise?"

Nikki took a sip of her coffee. "I can think of many times when you have." Nikki chuckled. "What could you possibly want from me at six thirty in the morning?"

"I don't know. Maybe a fresh piece of gossip I can send to the printer? How's it going?"

"Uh, I don't know how my father did this for so many years," Nikki wailed and sat at her desk again.

"Well, you've been doing the very same thing for the past twenty years, and you've been awesome." Veronica applauded her.

"You don't need to grovel." Nikki laughed. "I'm working on something. Or some things. We'll see what I come up with when I get there. But let me get back to work, please. Why are *you* up anyway?"

"I'm always up. You keep me busy," Veronica replied.

Nikki laughed. "See you later, Von."

She sank into her leather chair and stared at the computer screen. She wore her plush bathrobe like she did every morning. It was something of a routine for her— get up at five, brainstorm, research, drink coffee, brainstorm some more, and then go to work. By the time she clocked in, she'd already done half a day's work.

But she loved what she did. Journalism was in her blood. It was the one good thing her father gave her, and her spirit sank as she thought about him.

But that wasn't the only thought that crossed her mind, and her face soured when she remembered her good-for-nothing ex-husband, Josh Winden.

"I don't know how you do this every morning," he *would always tell her.*

"Easy. I pretend it's someone I'm trying to convict."

"Very funny," he *would say. "I thought you'd have gone on to some more respectable form of journalism."*

"You mean like being in the middle of a war zone reporting on casualties and prisoners of war and extreme political policies?" Nikki *asked and rolled her eyes as she often did. Josh had never liked the type of journalism she did, but it was what she loved. She didn't like seeing him*

deal with criminals all day long, but that was the life they chose. "You sound as if you didn't know what I did? I've been doing it for twenty years."

She blinked back the memories and tried to regain focus on her article.

Nikki gathered her documents, stuck them in a binder she kept for her current stories, and returned upstairs to get ready for work.

She made her way downtown to the office of the *The Arlington Times*, her home away from home for the past two decades. It was a busy morning as she navigated the traffic that was already picking up.

The air was cool, and the sun's early morning rays warmed the store awnings and pavement. Her office was located on the eighteenth floor of one of the skyscrapers in the metropolitan region of Arlington.

"Good morning, Miss Murphy," the security guard in the lobby called to her. His broad grin rivaled the sun.

"Hi, Gerry," she beamed in return. "Good day for a swim, huh?"

"Tell me about it." He laughed. "But someone's gotta look out for you."

"I appreciate it," she replied and hurried to the elevator. She wasn't late, but a story was brewing in her mind, and she didn't want to lose the creative spark.

She breezed past Holly, the receptionist who barely managed to throw a good morning her way. She tossed her bag onto the visitor's chair and started her laptop.

She was itching to start her story and hoped it would make the evening paper.

"What do we have?" Veronica asked as she appeared over Nikki's shoulder.

Nikki wheeled her chair excitedly and made a

sweeping gesture in the air as she stated her headline: **Judge Caught with his Pants Down!**

Veronica squealed and rubbed her palms together as if she'd never heard a piece of gossip before. "I love it!"

"Now shoo, so I can write it." Nikki motioned with her hand for Veronica to leave and returned to her computer screen.

"You've got it," Veronica replied, walking off, her red hair rubbing her shoulders as she returned to her office.

She was going over the story of a local judge who had aspirations of making it to the Supreme Court when his dreams were dashed by an unsuspecting maid who caught him cheating. He literally had his pants down, and the political spin-offs were just too juicy not to record.

She was typing what felt like a hundred words per minute when her phone rang. She ignored it. If she lost her train of thought, she'd lose her angle and forget something.

That was one of the reasons she tried to write in the early mornings when everything was quiet.

Nikki was halfway through the story when the phone rang again. "Come on," she wailed. Who could it be at that time of the morning? It was barely nine.

She kept tapping away, but when the phone rang for the third time, she lost it. She grabbed it, not even noticing the number or the name on the screen.

"Hello!" she said with great annoyance.

"Hello? Is this Nikki Murphy? Or Nikki Winden?"

Nikki paused and pulled the phone back to check who the caller was. It read: Frank Lynch. Suddenly, her whole world paused, and her story was forgotten.

"Mr. Lynch?" she asked timidly. He was the lawyer her parents had retained when she was growing up, and the last time he'd called her, eight years ago, was to tell her that her parents had been in an accident in Mexico while they'd been on vacation. They'd been out snorkeling and had gotten caught in a riptide that pulled them under. The vast amount of money and possessions that Nikki and Trish had inherited didn't do much to stay that measure of grief, and Nikki felt the familiar lump form in her throat all over again.

"Yes. Is this Nikki?" he asked again, just to make sure.

She gulped. "Yes, it is. What's wrong?"

She could almost feel it—the enormous sense of dread—and watched as goose pimples filled her arms.

"I'm sorry to be calling you at this dreadful hour of the day, but I'm afraid I have some bad news. It's your sister, Trish."

The tears started rolling down Nikki's face before he even relayed the bad news. "Please tell me she's okay."

Mr. Lynch cleared his throat. "She's been in a serious accident and has severe internal bleeding, so the doctors had to induce a coma to keep her alive."

He kept explaining things, but Nikki didn't hear any of them. Her heart felt like it was being squeezed to the point of bursting as the tears streamed down her face.

The last time she'd seen her sister had been at their parents' funeral and later at the reading of the will. They'd promised to keep in touch, but like the years before that, they'd returned to being distant relatives.

To hear of her demise was a huge blow for Nikki that left her paralyzed.

"Are you there?" She heard Mr. Lynch in the background.

"Y-yes," she stuttered and cleared her throat. "I'm here. How bad is it?"

"It's hard to predict, but the doctors say it's up to her now. You need to come to Camano Island right away. We need to discuss some business."

"Forget the business," Nikki fumed. "I need to see my sister."

"The business has to do with your sister," Mr. Lynch continued.

"She's not dead yet!" Nikki cried as her voice got louder.

"I understand, ma'am," Mr. Lynch said nervously yet with understanding. "If I could have done things any other way, I would have. I don't like this any more than you do."

Nikki sighed and dabbed her eyes with a tissue. "I know, I'm sorry. I'll be there first thing tomorrow."

"I'll see you then," he said and hung up.

It was difficult after that to complete the article, but Nikki struggled through it. It didn't take Veronica long to figure out something was wrong with her. Nikki told her briefly about what had happened with her sister right before she put in for a couple of days off.

She wasn't sure how long her trip to Camano Island would be, but she couldn't think about that. She got the rest of the day off and returned home, but she wasn't sure which was worse—being at work or being alone in her huge house, wandering aimlessly from room to room as the guilt washed over her.

Since Trish and her parents decided not to give her the baby, she hadn't spoken to them. She hadn't returned to Seattle. Then her parents had died, and now Trish. She and Josh had never adopted children, but they'd remained married, if even in a loveless marriage that ended up with him cheating on her for three years and impregnating someone else.

She'd rationalized that it was partly her fault for not being able to have children, and she cursed Trish silently at the time.

The hours ticked by, and before she knew it, it was evening. She thought nothing of it when the doorbell rang, and she dragged herself to the door.

She swung it open, only to see Ava, her best friend of over a decade, donning a big grin and holding up a bottle of wine. "It's girls' night!" she yelled, seconds before she noticed Nikki's tearstained cheeks and sunken eyes. "Uh-oh. What's wrong, honey?" she asked as her hands fell to her sides.

Nikki walked back into the house as Ava followed her. Her raven-black hair was pulled back at her nape, and it swished across her back as she walked.

"I totally forgot about tonight." Nikki sighed, then sank into the sofa. She curled her legs under her and pulled the cushion between her legs. "I got a call from Mr. Lynch today. Trish has been in a car accident, and she may not survive," she said as fresh tears emerged. "Ava, I haven't seen her in years, and now I may never talk to her again."

"Oh, honey," Ava muttered as she reached over and pulled Nikki into her arms. "I'm so sorry. I know you two didn't get along, but this is awful."

Nikki sobbed against her friend's shoulder. "I have to go there tomorrow. I don't know how long I'll be gone."

"Shush! Don't worry about that now. Your sister needs you. Have you eaten at all today?'

"Not really," Nikki replied. "I hadn't thought much about it."

"Okay, I'm going to order us some takeout," Ava said as she pulled away from Nikki.

"I can't lose her, Ava." Nikki sobbed. It was as if the tears wouldn't stop raining down, consuming Nikki in the process.

"You won't," Ava promised her. "You won't."

She pulled her in for another hug, but deep down, Nikki dreaded the worst.

Chapter Two

Trish's face became a staple in Nikki's mind after the grim revelation.

It was hard to imagine that she may end up being the only one left of her family if Trish succumbed to her wounds and she hadn't made any effort to reconnect with her sister.

She should have understood why Trish couldn't give her the baby and why her parents had refused. They could have done so many things differently, but that was all in the past. What mattered was what happened next.

A somber feeling followed Nikki as she arrived to the island, but when she arrived, an entirely different feeling welcomed her.

Nikki peered at the slow-moving Stillaguamish River below as she drove over the Camano Gateway Bridge. It brought back memories of the emerald-colored water that once reflected the hue of the evergreens that sandwiched it as it meandered its way toward Puget Sound. But with the construction of the new bridge a few years back, she could see that her memory of it had changed.

Coming upon the sign "Welcome to Camano Island" instantly teleported her to the days when her family rented summer homes there every year. Most of the island was busiest in the summertime, and her arrival was in stark contrast to the overall mood.

As she drove through downtown Camano, she watched tourists and locals walk up and down the streets lined with locally owned small businesses dwarfed by a few department stores, a mall, and business complexes. The air was salty and sweet at the same time, and all-around, she was invited to taste the ocean. She would have probably ventured into one of the seafood restaurants for the experience if not for the fact that she needed to get to her destination to see her sister.

Nikki made her way to the Nestled Inn that Trish owned, which was new information to her. She hadn't known her sister to have a business head, but then again, she didn't know much about her sister at all. The path to Trish's business was littered with childhood memories as she glanced through Camano's storefront windows.

She smiled faintly as she passed the antiquarian bookstore she had often visited when the summer days had gotten boring as a child. Old stone walls lined the byways, and summer's vibrant green and yellow colors weaved along the stones like a modern tapestry.

The general architecture was one of the old brick homes that gave the feeling one had traveled back in time.

She turned onto NE Camano Drive, where she saw lush woodlands broken up by unoccupied grassy lots, as well as gorgeous bungalows and two-story homes on spacious lots. The foliage thinned off to her left, revealing the blue ocean beyond. A more unobstructed vista of the big ocean opened up before her as she climbed Camano Hill Road. Glacier Peak Drive was the next street on the GPS route, so she took it and climbed the steep hill to reach Blue Mountain Road.

The houses along this stretch were much bigger and on magnificent lots of land. Even though the ocean was much farther away, she could taste the salt from the air, and once again, her thoughts switched to the fresh seafood available at the restaurants scattered throughout downtown and along the coast. Another thing to die for was the breathtaking view of the beautiful Cascade Mountains, which was like an art form on an exhibition with Mount Baker and Port Susan in the distance.

Her mind was in complete disarray by the time she arrived at the Nestled Inn, but its magnificence took her breath away. It was a great three-story wood and stone structure with gabled roofs and balconies on the second floor. Large French windows and doors finished the adorning of the beautiful building. She could see the adjoining restaurant named Lot 28 displayed on a plaque above the main door. There was also a house on the property next to the inn that Nikki assumed was part of the entire spread.

Nikki inhaled deeply as she walked into the establishment and was immediately greeted by an animated woman.

"You must be Nikki, Trish's sister," the rosy-cheeked woman said as she hurried to meet her. She had long chestnut hair and a runner's figure. She appeared middle-aged and spritely as she practically skipped to take Nikki's hand.

"I am," Nikki replied and looked around at the immaculately kept space. A large crystal chandelier hung above them, and modern paintings and soft-hue lights adorned the walls with a gentle ambiance. She instantly felt pride in the image before her.

"So good to meet you. I'm Kaylyn Morris, the manager and receptionist here, and this is Dorothy, head of housekeeping," she introduced as a woman who seemed roughly the same age as her joined them.

"Pleased to meet you, ma'am, and I'm so sorry for what happened to Miss Trish," she said sadly, and Kaylyn nodded in agreement.

"Thank you both," Nikki told them.

"Oh, let me show you to the main house where Miss Trish stays," Kaylyn said as she walked off. "We've already prepared everything for you, so if you need anything, just let us know."

"I don't know how to thank you enough," Nikki said as she followed the woman, but Kaylyn kept turning around to face her when she spoke.

"It's no worry," Kaylyn replied. "We love Trish, and we hope she comes around soon. It's such an awful thing that happened. I hope they catch that crook who ran into her."

Nikki didn't even want to consider the specifics of the crash. She needed to get situated and get to the hospital right away. "I hope so too."

"I was told to show you around. The Nestled Inn has six bedrooms, which can accommodate twelve adults at any time."

Kaylyn took her down the hall and up the stairs, where she was shown the available rooms. Two were occupied, but Nikki had a pretty good idea of what they'd look like. She had to admit the place was exquisite and homey, unlike some of the inns she was familiar with, where you just slept in and left as soon as possible. At the Nestled Inn, you wanted to stay.

She was sorry she couldn't enjoy it more.

When they finished the tour, Kaylyn showed her the restaurant. "This is the sister restaurant to the other Lot 28, which is a one Michelin star restaurant," Kaylyn beamed with pride.

"She has a one Michelin star restaurant?" Nikki asked as her eyes popped.

"The whole place is a five-star experience," Kaylyn beamed. "I mean, sure, it didn't start that way, but then Paul came along and helped her turn this place around. He sort of co-joined with her so she could take his brand, and here we are," Kaylyn said as she opened the door to the house.

"That's incredible," Nikki remarked. "I had no idea."

Kaylyn nodded. "Paul should be coming by shortly, but make yourself at home," Kaylyn said. "I'll be back at the desk if you need anything."

"Thank you, Kaylyn," Nikki gushed. "I appreciate you."

"My pleasure," Kaylyn said, then retreated.

Nikki walked slowly into the space, already feeling lousy. She had never been there, and it pained her that she had missed so much of her sister's life—twenty-one years of it. She set her bags by the door and walked around the room.

Nikki could sense her sister's presence as she wandered over to the mantel and picked up pictures of when she was younger. Nikki felt the pull on her heart-strings, and she choked on the invisible lump that had formed in her throat.

It was hard as she smelled the throw draped across the

sofa or wandered into the kitchen and smelled the faint scent of coffee lingering in the air. Fresh tears rolled down her cheeks, and she swiftly brushed them away moments before a knock sounded on the door.

She knitted her brows as she returned to the door and pulled it open. She gasped when she saw who it was. "Paul?"

"Nikki," he said as a wide grin developed on his face.

Before she could say another word, she was in his arms, and he hugged her and lifted her off the ground like an old friend. "You're the Paul who Kaylyn mentioned?" Nikki asked in disbelief.

"I am," he said and entered the house. "It's a pity we have to reunite under such sad circumstances."

"Yeah," Nikki replied. She had dated Paul all through high school, but they'd broken up when she'd left for college. She hadn't seen him since, but he had aged well. "You look good, Paul." He had a more distinguished face. He wore a few days-old face stubble, and his black hair had streaks of gray running through it. His gray eyes were warm and kind and danced when he smiled.

"Right back at you," he told her. "Listen, about Trish..."

"Right," Nikki replied as she gathered her wits. "I need to get to the hospital. I haven't been to see her yet."

"Okay. I can take you if you'd like," he offered. "I just came by to check on you and to see if you needed anything. I can't imagine how hard this must be for you."

"I'm glad you and Trish found each other," Nikki said gratefully. "I'd hate to think she was out here all alone."

"Yeah, when she came back here, we sort of bumped into each other accidentally. I was sad to hear she hadn't heard from you in a while, but when I realized she owned this place, I stuck around to make sure she was okay and helped her out when I could."

"Oh, really?"

"Yeah. We reconnected and became fast friends. I saw how I could help her by suggesting she change the restaurant's name. People already knew about Lot 28 and would expect the same quality service here. She'd pick up business better, and it worked," he said as he widened his arms. "I was just happy she wasn't too proud to accept the offer, but we've been somewhat of partners since then."

"That was awfully nice of you, Paul." Nikki smiled. "I wouldn't expect anything different from you. You were always a white knight." She remembered that about him from her high school days. "It may not be necessary, but thanks for everything. I haven't been around, but it's good to know she was in good company."

"She was." Paul smiled. "Everyone around here loves her. And you know, you can always call me, just like she could."

"I might be calling you a lot. I haven't been to Camano in years."

Paul chuckled. "Nothing's changed. You'll get the hang of things. How long are you staying?"

"It all depends on how well Trish is doing. And then there's that business with the lawyer that I still haven't figured out."

"Oh right," Paul said, but Nikki got the impression he knew exactly what she was talking about. "When do you meet with him?"

"Tomorrow. I'm not sure what that's about because she isn't dead," Nikki said and gulped again.

"No, and you won't think like that either." Paul

touched her shoulder gently. "She's a fighter, and she will pull through. I have no doubt about that."

Nikki desperately wanted to believe that, but she feared the worst. "I'll take you up on that offer to go to the hospital, but please, come back after my visit with Trish so we can catch up and," she said, gesticulating at the establishment, "get familiar with all of this."

"Sure thing." Paul smiled. "How are you holding up?"

"I could be better." Nikki sighed. "I don't think I'll be okay until she is."

"Understood." Paul checked his watch. "Maybe we should get going."

"Yeah, right," Nikki agreed as she followed Paul out of the house.

She was in a familiar place that was also strange and different at the same time. She'd spent entire summers on Camano Island growing up, but somehow, it was like walking into a foreign country. Everything was different, and she was alone.

And as they approached the Camano Hospital, she couldn't help thinking that her whole life was about to change.

Chapter Three

The feeling of melancholy followed them on the short trip.

They hardly spoke a word as the car rolled along. Nikki kept her eyes trained on the slow-moving pedestrians and life carrying on as usual.

A slight wind wafted toward her, bringing the smell of fish, salt, and sand to her. She could hear the crashing of waves in the distance. The Camano Hospital was a giant among minions when Paul pulled up outside the front entrance.

"I'll see you later," he said as she got out.

She nodded as words escaped her. It was as if being closer to Trish gave her a greater sense of dread, and as she walked toward the nursing station, goose pimples raced up and down her arms, and the hair at her nape stood on end.

"Hi, how can I help you?" the nurse asked as she looked up at Nikki.

It felt like déjà vu for her, in a sense. "Uh, yes. I was

wondering which room Trish Murphy is in. She was in an accident yesterday."

She waited for what felt like forever as the golden-haired nurse clicked away at the computer keys. "Trish Murphy. Yes. She's in room 303."

"Thank you," Nikki said and walked off. She moved toward the elevator, but it didn't feel like she was in control of her body. She felt like an automaton, and it grew increasingly worse when she exited the elevator on the third floor.

Her hand shook when she turned the knob to room 303. When she entered and saw Trish, with her head bandaged and tubes running from her nose and mouth, Nikki's legs gave way as she broke down by the door. She clutched the wall as her emotions overtook her until she felt a morsel of strength return to her. She lumbered over to the bed and clung to the bed rail as she stared at her sister's likeness.

Nothing there resembled Trish. She had tubes coming out of her mouth, nose, and arms. Machines were connected to her, beeping constantly but keeping her alive. Nikki had to stare hard to see the rising and falling of her chest through her shallow breathing.

It was a hard scene to take in, and Nikki collapsed onto the chair when the doctor came in.

"Hello, I'm Dr. McCarthy," he said and held out his hand to Nikki.

She wiped her left hand across her face and reached for his hand. "I'm Nikki. Trish's sister. How is she?"

She asked the question but wasn't sure she was prepared for the answer. "Right now, her prognosis isn't good, I'm afraid to say. Her right leg is broken, her face has a lot of cuts and bruises from the shattered windshield, and she suffered a severe brain bleed, which forced us to induce a coma to keep her alive. We're doing everything we can to bring the swelling down and to contain the bleeding, but as of right now, there's nothing we can do," he said as the wrinkles at his eyes twitched with concern. "It's up to her now."

Nikki started crying again. He was right. The situation seemed hopeless. "So there's nothing to do but wait?"

"I'm afraid so." The doctor smiled weakly. "I'm sorry I couldn't give you better news. I've seen patients wake up from worse situations, so don't give up on her just yet."

Nikki nodded, and the doctor left the room. The ominous beeping was discouraging as she sat by the bedside and took Trish's hand in hers. She stroked the back of her hand as she remembered the argument they'd had so very long ago when she was nineteen and pregnant. They'd never been close, and Nikki couldn't understand why, but none of that mattered anymore.

She was there, and she prayed Trish would awaken so she could tell her what an idiot she'd been. Then she remembered what medical experts had always said regarding coma patients—that they sometimes could hear what was going on around them even though they couldn't respond.

"Trish, if you can hear me," she said with a shaky voice, "it's Nikki." She burst into tears again. "I'm so sorry." She sobbed. "I should have been there for you all this time. I was so mad at you and Mom and Dad, and I wasn't thinking, and now, I can't even remember why I was so angry with you for so long."

She laid her head against Trish's hip as her body rocked with pain. "I've never asked you for anything, Trish. I've never needed anything, but I need something right now that only you can give me," she said and lifted her face to stare at her sister's still countenance. "I need you to wake up." She squeezed Trish's hand. "Please. Just wake up."

Nikki sobbed and replaced her head on her sister's hip and closed her eyes as the tears refused to stop. She had never known that much pain until that moment, and as if in defense, she drifted off into a short sleep.

She startled herself awake a couple of minutes later, surprised that she'd dozed off. The loud beeping continued in the background, but there was no point in remaining through the night. The doctors weren't hopeful she'd awaken soon, but until then, Nikki would be where Trish needed her most.

She might be in Camano longer than she'd planned.

Nikki called a cab to drop her off at Trish's house, and as soon as she returned, she climbed into the hot tub. It soothed her body and washed away some of the melancholic feelings.

Half an hour later, she climbed out and donned her sister's bathrobe. It made her feel closer to Trish and comforted Nikki in a small way.

Paul showed up later that evening, which was a welcomed visit. She didn't want to be alone with her thoughts, and she was happy to have a familiar face she could rely on.

He told her to relax while he whipped up something for them to eat. It turned out to be grilled salmon, asparagus, and garlic mashed potatoes.

"Wow," Nikki exclaimed when he presented the dish. "You made this?"

Paul knitted his brows. "You know I'm a chef, right?"

"Oh right, Lot 28," Nikki said. "Forgive me."

He chuckled. "Nothing to forgive." He sat on the barstool next to her by the kitchen island as she picked at the meal. It tasted great, and the salmon melted in her mouth like butter, but she wasn't of the mind to appreciate it as she should.

"How did the accident happen?" Nikki asked as she slid a stalk of asparagus around her plate.

"From what the police report says, she was slammed from behind, and the force of the impact pushed her into a utility pole. The car sort of wrapped around it. The guy was speeding," Paul reported. "He didn't make it, unfortunately, and now Trish is fighting for her life because of it."

Nikki's heart grew heavy again after he gave her the rundown. "Wow."

"That's the simple way to put it," Paul agreed.

"What was she like?" She kept her head down as she stared at the plate. She couldn't believe she had to ask that question about her own sister.

"She was great," Paul told her. "Everyone loved her. She was kind and giving. She volunteers at the Humane Society. She is so into animals, but she didn't get one for herself. She is a member of the board, but she's always giving to the community in one way or another. As you can imagine, everyone is rooting for her to pull through."

"I can imagine." Nikki sighed.

"You know, with Trish out for the moment, the board hopes you'll fill in until she returns. Trish was a big part of this huge event they've been planning for next week."

"I'll do it," Nikki said right away.

Paul chuckled. "Really? They'll be delighted to hear that."

"I'll do anything I can while I'm here and for as long as I'm needed."

"What about your job?" Paul asked with concern.

"I'm a journalist. I can write from anywhere," she reminded him.

"It's settled then," he said and leaned forward on the counter. "I'll let them know."

Nikki nodded, happy that she was able to help in some small way.

Nikki's curiosity got the better of her when she arrived at Frank Lynch's office the following day.

"I have to admit I'm a little curious about why I'm here," she said as the man directed her to the leather chair facing him.

He'd aged a little since the last time she'd seen him, but he still appeared stately, only showing signs of his aging at his temples. His face was solemn and sincere yet gentle, and she appreciated his calmness.

"This shouldn't take long, but I'll get into it to ease your concerns." He smiled at her over the rim of his glasses.

Nikki was practically balancing on the edge of her seat. When her parents had died, they'd left them with six figures each and a substantial amount of property, stocks, and investments. She didn't need enrichment from the passing of her sister. What she wanted was her sister to wake up.

Frank opened a folder on his desk, straightened his glasses, and proceeded to read from it. "In the event of her passing, and I'm just summing this up," he clarified as he looked up at her, "the Nestled Inn will pass onto you and Amy Foster."

Nikki narrowed her eyes. "Amy Foster?"

"Yes. Her daughter," Frank replied.

"Daughter? She has a daughter?" she asked in wonderment. How much had she missed?

"It's the daughter she gave up for adoption over twenty years ago that she's been trying to find. She hired a private investigator, but at the time of the accident, they hadn't furnished a report yet."

"Wow," Nikki exclaimed.

Frank waited for any further questions before he continued. "What she wants is for you to follow up with the investigation, with the help of Paul Thompson, to track down Amy Foster and for the two of you to build a relationship and partner in running the Nestled Inn here in Camano."

"This is incredible," Nikki said as her jaw dropped at Frank's revelation. She was to find the child she'd always wanted.

"If you choose to give up your claims to the Nestled Inn, it is her wish that you'd run it with Amy, on the condition you do find her, for at least a year, after which you can sell her your shares and move on. She also wishes that Paul remains on staff—he can't be fired." Frank looked up at her and closed the file to indicate he was done. "Those are her wishes, and I know I don't need to ask your opinions, but her intentions have been made known. How you choose to proceed is your choice."

"Thank you," Nikki replied. "With any luck, she'll awaken, and I won't need to worry about any of it."

"Agreed," Frank said.

"I guess if that's all, then," Nikki said as she stood. Frank did as well, and the two shook hands.

Nikki left the office with a lot to contemplate. She'd come to Camano to be with her sister and help nurse her back to health if needed, but it turned out she would be living her sister's life.

She wasn't sure for how long, but she was determined to do her best to give Trish what she should have all those years.

She just wasn't sure how well she could do it.

Chapter Four

The following day didn't get any easier for Nikki. She got up early and readied herself, hopeful that the new day would bring good news. That was not the case. When she walked into the hospital room, Trish lay as lifeless as she had the day before.

Nikki's heart sank. She stood over her bed as fresh guilt washed over her, and before she could break down again, she hurried out of the room. She couldn't just stay by the bed and watch her die. Or at least, she hoped that wasn't what she would be doing.

Her heart was heavy when she returned to the Nestled Inn. She had a lot to get done, and she didn't have the faintest idea where to begin. She was relieved when she returned and saw Paul behind the desk with Kaylyn.

"There you are," he greeted her warmly and rounded the oval wooden partition to meet her. "How are you holding up?"

Nikki sighed. "I don't even know. I just need something to do, or I'll go crazy. Hey, Kaylyn," she called when she realized she'd completely ignored the woman. "I'm sorry, my head's all over the place."

"It's alright, ma'am." She smiled. "I understand."

"We have plenty for you to do," Paul told her. "Come with me."

"I already gave her a tour of the businesses and house," Kaylyn told him. "And she met Dorothy too."

"Oh, okay," Paul said and scratched his head. "On to business, then. Follow me."

Nikki walked after him to a door next to the reception area that housed an office. Paul showed her inside and closed the door after him. It was an ample enough space with a large desk in the center filled with stacks of files and a stationery holder. A desktop computer and a laptop nested on the front of the desk. Paul motioned to the leather chair for her to take a seat.

"Oh no, go ahead," Nikki told him. "I'm not the boss yet. As of now, that's still you." She smiled.

Paul laughed, and the sound bounced off the walls. Nikki couldn't believe how good he looked still. She hadn't seen him for so long, yet it felt like it was only the day before. "I don't know about that. I'll help out."

"Seems like more to me," Nikki said and collapsed into the chair opposite him.

He steepled his fingers under his chin and stared at her. "You look good. How have you been?"

"I can't complain." She smiled. "Been at the *Providence Journal* since I started working. I don't know anything else, and you know how much I love it."

"Don't I?" He chuckled. "You broke up with me to chase that dream. I'm glad to see it wasn't a phase, or I would have been upset."

Nikki laughed. "Yeah. And what about you? You're a chef, but then, I shouldn't be surprised. You always loved cooking, but one Michelin star?" she said, tapping his arm playfully. "Look at you."

"I guess we're both very good at what we do." He smiled.

"Trish didn't seem to have done badly for herself either," Nikki said as she looked around the office at the pictures of Trish and some of the townspeople at various events, community awards she'd received that were snug in the curio by the small bookshelf, and a couple of single ones of her, smiling.

Nikki picked up a picture frame from off the desk. "I've missed her even though I didn't want to admit it to myself. I was just so angry all those years. I couldn't understand why they wouldn't just let me have the baby." She turned to look at him. "Did she tell you any of that? About what happened back then?"

Paul shook his head. "She told me some."

"She told you about her daughter? How she wouldn't give her to me? And after all this time, her lawyer called me," she said and inched closer to Paul. "I don't understand why I was asked to be here other than to visit her. Did she tell you anything about the will?"

"A little," he replied. "But I'll wait until after you've spoken to Mr. Lynch."

Nikki sighed. She remembered enough about Paul to know she wouldn't get much more out of him. She would have to wait a little more, as agonizing as it was.

Nikki inhaled sharply before she plastered a smile onto her face. "So," she asked, spreading her arms, "what do I need to know? How do I run a business?"

Paul laughed and handed her a file with the latest

numbers and current guest registry.

"What do I do with these?" Nikki asked. She'd always been a journalist, so she had no idea what to do with a business. "Are you sure you don't want to do this without me?"

"I don't even run my own business alone." Paul laughed.

"How come?" Nikki asked curiously.

He waved her off. "It's nothing. I had a heart attack a couple of years ago, so I try to take it easy now. But enough about me. I'll give you the rundown of the business, who does what, and how to conduct affairs. I'll oversee the restaurant."

"I'm sorry to hear that," she said.

"It is what it is, I guess," he said nonchalantly, but she figured he didn't want to go into the details right then.

Nikki listened attentively while he described everything he had said earlier. She couldn't say she understood all of it, but she was eager to do as much as she could for her sister.

"This will take some getting used to," Nikki said when Paul closed the file and rocked back in the chair.

"You'll get the hang of it." He stood. "Now, how about some lunch? I doubt you've had anything to eat all morning, and there's a one Michelin star dining experience next door."

Nikki's stomach rumbled just then in agreement, and she blushed. "You're right. I could eat."

"Let's go then," Paul said and led her back into the lobby. "Kaylyn, we'll be out for a couple of hours."

"That's alright," the woman replied.

Nikki couldn't say she had ever gone to a restaurant with a Michelin star. She was bedazzled when she entered Lot 28, the restaurant Paul owned. The place reeked of class and stateliness, and she doubted she could have even afforded the appetizer if she had gone alone.

Even the menu cards had black and gold lace trimmings to resemble the swirling patterns on the walls. Everything displayed the same theme, even the cutlery on the tables, which stood out against the off-white table linen.

"Paul, I'm...wow," Nikki said as she clutched her chest. "I'm at a loss for words."

"Right this way," he said, leading her to a private table with a *reserved* card. He pulled the chair out for her, and she sat gingerly like she thought she might fall through it.

She was about to reach for the menu card when he swiped it. "It's the chef's special for you today." He winked at her. "Be right back."

A server came by shortly to offer her a glass of white wine. She wasn't even sure what brand it was, but it didn't matter. She was already loving the experience, and she hadn't even had her meal yet.

That turned out to be braised scallops as an appetizer, followed by beef Wellington served with sweet potato puree, fingerling potatoes, and fresh herbs. Paul wanted her to try the soufflé, but she was too full.

"I could get used to this," she said and sank back in the chair when she finished eating.

"This will be your life for the rest of the time you're here," he said.

One of the servers hastily approached them with a worried look and whispered something to Paul. His brows knitted, and he turned to Nikki. "Will you be okay getting back to the Nestled Inn on your own? There's something I need to attend to. Or if you'd like to stick around—"

"No, it's fine." Nikki stopped him. "Thank you for the meal. I absolutely loved it, but it has been an overwhelming day. I need some relaxation time."

"Okay. I'll check in on you later."

Paul hurried away, and with nothing else to do, Nikki got up and left. Her eyes were getting heavy by the time she got back, but Kaylyn ran up to her as soon as she walked inside.

"Ma'am, someone's been here asking for you," she said.

Nikki's brows dipped. "Someone? Who?" She couldn't imagine who it could be and could only assume it had to do with Trish.

"A young woman," she replied. "She said she knows you from Arlington."

Nikki was even more intrigued. "What does she look like?"

"Nikki!"

Nikki wheeled around just in time to see Ava with her arms spread and her face glowing. "Ava? What are you doing here?" She laughed as she ran into her friend's embrace.

"Hey, you didn't think I'd let you come here and have all the fun, did you?"

"I don't know what your idea of fun is." Nikki laughed. She turned to Kaylyn. "Her?"

The woman nodded. "I can see that you're friends."

"Yes. Ava, this is Kaylyn, the manager. Kaylyn, this is my best friend, Ava, who I assume will be staying a couple of days as well."

"Nice to meet you," they said simultaneously and then laughed.

"I'll leave you two alone," Kaylyn said, returning to her post.

"This place is great," Ava said as she turned around. "Not your average inn."

"No, indeed. Trish did really good," Nikki said with a sigh.

Ava grabbed her forearm and turned Nikki around to face her. "How is she?"

"She's being kept alive by machines and a force of will," Nikki said with a heavy heart.

"Aw," Ava said and hugged her. "I'm so sorry, hun."

"I know," Nikki replied.

"But that's also why I'm here. I couldn't let you do this alone. What are friends for, right?"

"Thanks, Ava."

"You've got it, kiddo." Ava smiled. "Where do I put these?" she asked, indicating her bags.

"I'm staying in Trish's apartment. You can too," Nikki invited her, and the two women headed in that direction.

Ava was animated for the entire time. She had only been to Camano a couple of times, but that was years ago. She couldn't wait to go surfing and get a tan on the beach.

It didn't take Ava long to get situated, but it was hard for Nikki to hide the swirling emotions inside her.

"She's going to be okay," Ava reassured her as the two sat on the sofa watching a movie. Nikki barely saw anything happening.

"I know," she said sadly. "I just don't know how we got here. We were closer when we were younger, but somehow, we drifted apart over the years until we were practically strangers. I used to think that was why she wouldn't let me have the baby—that she had said no out of spite."

"Oh, honey, I don't think that was true," Ava replied empathetically. "She was young and confused, I'm sure."

"Perhaps," Nikki said and wiped her hand down her face. "Regardless, it was her decision. My inability to have children wasn't her fault, and I could have adopted another child. I shouldn't have been so angry with her and my parents for years because of it, and now, I could lose my entire family, and they don't even know how sorry I am," she said as tears ran down her face.

Ava wiped the tears from the corners of her eyes and embraced Nikki as she shushed her. "It's going to be fine. She'll wake up, and then you can tell her," she consoled.

Nikki could barely respond. She nodded as she clung to her friend and soaked the shoulder of her blouse with her tears.

She was drained afterward, and they both decided to retreat to their beds. Nikki lay on her back, staring at the ceiling. She had made so many mistakes in her life, but she needed a loving voice, and it was interesting that Paul's face came to mind.

Ever since the divorce, she'd struggled with dating. She'd gone on blind dates and traditional dates, but none had lasted. She knew she could attribute much of that to a lack of ability to trust anyone like she had with Josh.

Even his name in her head sparked bitterness still, but she quickly squelched it with thoughts of her sister and why she was in town. The divorce was three years ago, but its effect was still fresh despite her strength of character.

She would just have to find other ways to deal with her repressed feelings. Maybe she should date again, and for a fleeting moment, she wondered if Paul might be up for it.

Chapter Five

Paul didn't want to leave Nikki alone when she was already so low, but he had just found out one of his line cooks was threatening to quit.

"What's going on?" he asked as he entered the kitchen.

"I can't work with Ken," Will complained, and the veins in his forehead bulged. "He doesn't listen."

"You're the one who doesn't listen," Ken shouted.

"Hey!" Paul yelled at them both. "In case neither of you realized, this isn't a preschool playground. I'm trying to run a reputable business here, and I didn't get this far to have my main guys bickering like schoolgirls. Get your act together and start doing your jobs," he told them.

"Ken, you're the sous chef for a reason. I expect you to lead, not dictate. Will, he is your superior. A little respect goes a long way. What's this talk about quitting?"

"Never mind." Will shook his head. "It was a misunderstanding."

"Is that so?" Paul turned to Ken. "What do you say?"

"It's nothing. We're cool," he said, wiping the towel down his face.

"Great. Now, we have a dining room full of guests waiting to be served. I suggest you both get back to it. You're good at what you do. Now act like it!"

The men nodded and returned to work. That afternoon bled into an even busier Friday evening, and Paul found himself staying at the restaurant into the busy hours. Once or twice, he joined the kitchen staff in preparing dinner tickets, but nothing too strenuous.

He was entering the dining room after preparing what he figured was his last ticket of the day when he noticed a waving Sarah by the door.

She was the spitting image of her mother, and Paul's face lit up as he hurried over to her. "Hey, kiddo." He lifted her off the ground in a tight squeeze.

"Dad," she said, punching his arm playfully. "Not here." She laughed. "And watch your back."

"It's not my back you need to worry about," he said as he set her down. "It's my heart that you're going to break for taking so long to visit."

She laughed. "Are you busy now? Please tell me you're not still manning the line back there."

He glanced back in the direction of the kitchen staff. "No, you know I can't handle all of that. Not since the heart attack. Here, let's go out on the patio."

He pushed the door outward, and they sat under the umbrella covering the table on the patio. It was a beautiful, clear night where the stars were visible, and the ocean rolling in the background was like a live photo.

"I'll never get tired of this," Sarah said as the gentle breeze toyed with her dark-brown hair and tossed it across her face. She was sweeping it behind her ear when she caught her father staring at her. "What?"

"I can't believe how much you look like her," Paul said as he remembered his wife. She had died ten years ago from leukemia, and the memory of it still cut like a knife, especially when Sarah was around.

He struggled to be a single parent after that, and Sarah went through bouts of rebellion that drove him up the wall. He constantly felt like a failure, but then, almost overnight, she blossomed into a woman he could be proud of, and he was. She was also struggling with the loss of her mother, but somewhere, through their grief, they reconnected.

"Sometimes I pretend she's still here." Sarah sighed.

"That's really healthy," Paul quipped, raising his brows.

She giggled, and he spotted the deep dimples in her cheeks. "I mean, I like thinking of her like she isn't just...gone."

"Yeah, I know what you mean," he said to her and sat back in the chair. "I think the shock of it was what gave me the heart attack in the first place. I don't think it was working here. I love doing this."

"I know," Sarah said as she stared at the ocean. "I couldn't have handled losing the two of you."

"Hey," Paul said as he took her hand across the table. "I'm not going anywhere. But, even if I did, you already found a replacement."

"Don't talk like that," Sarah scolded. "And Aaron is not a replacement. He's the other man I love."

Paul laughed. "The other man."

"Yes!" She laughed. "But don't tell him I said that."

"How is he, by the way?"

"Uh, he's okay, I guess. He's been busy picking up night shifts at the hospital. I've tried to avoid those, but I guess it's okay for now. I wouldn't want him doing that when we decide to have a family."

Paul's brows shot up. "Is there talk of that? So soon?"

"Don't worry, Dad." She laughed. "I won't make you a grandfather just yet."

"Phew!" he teased. "Although I can't say I'd mind a rug rat or two crawling all over me. It would give me something else to do now that I'm not here as much anymore."

"And how's that working out?" Sarah followed up and leaned forward.

A server came onto the patio, and Paul called him over and ordered a bottle of Dom Perignon.

"Oh, classy," Sarah teased and wiggled her fingers. "But back to the restaurant. I was worried you'd lose your Michelin rating or something when you stepped away."

"To be honest," he said and leaned forward secretly, "I was a little anxious about that too. But Francois is doing an amazing job. The chefs, Will and Ken...superb." He kissed his steepled fingers. "I mean, they bicker from time to time, but they manage to send out amazing dishes every time. I can literally walk away to help Trish without worrying."

"I can see that." Sarah smiled as pride radiated on her face. "Is she going to be alright? I like her."

"I hope so." Paul sighed as he thought about her. "I didn't know she and I would have gotten along that well."

"Yeah," Sarah said. "For a second, I thought you two were going to be an item."

"Never crossed my mind," he said as nostalgia washed over him. "I saw what she was trying to do with the inn, but knowing the town folks as much as I did, I knew she'd have a hard time. She had some good ideas, but her execution wasn't always on point, and I had more experience, so I offered what help I could."

"You did way more than that," Sarah noted. "You gave her your restaurant's name. That was a big risk. What if she had flopped?"

Paul laughed. "I wasn't thinking about that at the time. But it worked. I wanted her to piggyback off Lot 28's reputation."

"That was a good thing you did, though." Sarah smiled. "I'm proud of you."

"Thanks, kiddo," he said as they sipped from their glasses and looked out at the pale silhouette of the horizon. "About you..." Paul said and tapped her arm. "I can't believe my little girl is going to get married."

"Yeah." She blushed and looked at the princess-cut diamond on her finger. "I can't believe it either. I was so surprised when he asked."

"I wasn't. He would have been crazy not to." Paul grinned.

Sarah sighed. "I just wish Mom could have been here for the wedding."

"I know." Paul sighed. "I wish she were here too, but you'll have to do it with just me."

Sarah smiled. "I can live with that. I know Aaron is fond of you. Speaking of which, I wonder how he's doing on his rounds. He's doubling tonight."

"That's why I'm not a nurse. I'm a cook. I work during sane hours," Paul teased.

"Well, luckily for you, there are people like us who work insane hours when you need us," she said and stuck out her tongue like a child.

He laughed. "I was just messing with you. In fact, I think it's great that he's a nurse. The medical field needs more men like that."

"You can say that again," Sarah agreed. "What are your plans for the rest of the night?"

Paul scratched his head. "I didn't really have any plans. I brought Nikki here for lunch and then..."

"Nikki?" Sarah asked with sudden intrigue.

"Don't get any ideas." He chuckled. "She's Trish's sister, although we used to have a thing back in high school."

"Oh, you did?" Sarah asked, and Paul could see the wheels turning in her head. "Is she pretty?"

"Sarah, I know you're happy with Aaron, but that doesn't mean you should start with the matchmaking. It's never worked before," Paul said and downed the rest of his glass of wine.

"But this time, it's an old flame. Is she single?"

"Yes, but it doesn't matter. We aren't thinking about that," he told her flatly.

"Speak for yourself," Sarah goaded. "She might be interested."

"What we had was decades ago. What are the odds we'd reconnect now?"

Sarah shrugged. "Who knows why anything happens?"

"You're right," he said and looked around. "But don't get your hopes up."

"Okay, but I can't promise you anything." Sarah giggled. "Anyway, I think I need to get going. I had a long day, and I want to put my feet up," she said.

"That makes two of us," Paul agreed as he pushed his chair back. "Let me walk you to your car."

They walked slowly toward the parking lot, the wind whistling in his ears. The air was crisp and salty, just the way he liked it. That was one of the reasons he'd moved to Camano after he'd completed his education. He loved the dynamic flair of the place and the uniqueness of the individual villages.

The people were warm and friendly, and he quickly grew attached to the place.

"So," Sarah said when she got to the car, "I'll come and see you soon."

"Should I believe you this time?" Paul asked and moved a wisp of hair from her face.

"Yes!" she said emphatically. "Unless I get extra busy, in which case I deserve a pass and a lot of forgiveness."

Paul laughed and hugged her. "Take care of yourself, will you?"

"I will," she said.

He watched as she got into her Chevy Cruze and pulled away. She honked the car on her way out, and Paul waved, then walked back toward the restaurant.

Her words didn't leave his mind as quickly as she had. He hadn't seen Nikki in years, but there was still a strong sense of familiarity with her. Sarah was right. What were the odds that she'd shown up in his life again, and at the most convenient time, when they were both single? Serendipity?

Paul didn't want to read too much into fate and circumstances, but as he walked back into the restaurant, he couldn't help feeling that there may be something to what Sarah had said after all.

And a smile spread across his face. It would not be the worst thing that could happen to him.

Chapter Six

"This town is like a dream," Ava said as she and Nikki returned from their morning run. "Why don't I live here?"

Nikki laughed. "I practically lived here all my summers growing up."

"Lucky you," Ava told her.

"It's not that different from Arlington if what you love are the beaches," Nikki told her. "There's plenty of that there."

They got back to the room and ordered breakfast because neither wanted to go out.

"Hey, remember the event with the Humane Society I told you about?" Nikki asked as she tilted her head sideways to dry her hair with the towel.

"Yeah," Ava replied. "It's that community outreach thing to raise money for the shelter."

"Right—*Furs are Friends.*" Nikki smiled. "I can understand in a sense why Trish and I never got along. We are so different."

"I can see that because no way would you have joined

a society like that," Ava said.

"I know, right? Yet here I am, and it's not even so bad," Nikki admitted. "I've always loved animals from a distance, but working so closely with them, I can see the appeal."

"Is it all about animals?" Ava wanted to know.

"No," Nikki said, sitting next to Ava. "It's more about a better quality of life for everyone, including animals. Today's event is all about the animals, though, so they have a competition lined up for the best-dressed dog, the best show dog, the purest breed, and stuff like that."

"That sounds like fun." Ava smiled. "Wish I had a dog to enter."

"There will be other activities. You can go into the dunk tank." Nikki grinned.

"Uh, me? At my age?" Ava scoffed. "Although I don't look so bad in a bikini. Maybe one of the...help...might take a fancy to me," she said and patted her hair flirtatiously.

Nikki erupted into laughter. "Some things never change, do they?"

"I'm guessing it's going to be by the beach? I hope so," Ava said.

"Yes, by Camano Island State Park. I remember going there as a child," Nikki said nostalgically.

"I can see how much you love this place." Ava smiled seconds before there was a knock on the door. "I wonder who that is."

Nikki had an idea. There weren't many people who knew her. She was pleasantly surprised when she saw Paul. "Hi," she said. "Come on in."

"Oh, who do we have here?" Ava said as she got up and fluffed her hair.

Paul laughed. "Paul," he said and extended his arm.

Ava looked over at Nikki quickly. "*The* Paul?"

Paul narrowed his eyes. "What does that mean?"

"Ignore her. This is my best friend, Ava," Nikki replied.

"Pleasure's all mine," Paul said and then immediately looked at Nikki. "Do you need help getting to the venue?"

"No, I have the rental," Nikki replied with a smile. "But thanks."

Paul nodded. "I'll see you there, then."

"Nice meeting you," Ava called as he headed through the door. "Wow," she said as soon as the door closed. "You mentioned there was a Paul back in the day but...wow."

"Yeah." Nikki blushed. "He's just a friend now, though. High school was years ago, and I was the one who walked away."

"So?" Ava asked as she came around the sofa. "He's still super cute."

"I know, but let's focus on the event," Nikki said and walked to the kitchen.

"How's Trish doing? I'm sorry I couldn't go with you this morning."

"It's okay." Nikki sighed. "There's nothing much to see, and you've gone with me for a couple of days now. Nothing's changed." Nikki sat on the barstool by the island. "Nothing except finding Amy."

"Her long-lost daughter," Ava said.

"Yes," Nikki said and wiped her hand down her face. "I know it's something I must do, but I'm a little anxious about it. What if I find her, and she doesn't want anything to do with Trish for giving her up? Or me?"

"Well, don't worry about that now," Ava consoled her. "You can't control any of that. All you can do is try.

Clearly, Trish wasn't worried about that. Maybe Amy will be over the moon."

"You think?" Nikki asked as her spirit slowly lifted.

"Yeah, don't worry about it. She's grown now. Who wouldn't want an aunt like you or a mother like Trish?" Ava smiled.

"I hope you're right."

"I am. So chin up, and let's get ready to have some fun."

Nikki was in much better spirits when they pulled up at the venue. The air was festive with music from the local band, laughter, dogs barking, and children cavorting all over the mossy green. Kiosks were set up all over, and various vendors displayed food and keepsakes.

Barbecue grills were smoking, and it felt a lot like being at a carnival. "I haven't been to anything like this in forever," Nikki observed as she walked toward the booth sheltering members of the Humane Society.

"Oh, bingo," Ava said as she veered to the right.

Nikki laughed. "I'll catch up with you later."

Three members were at the booth, including Reed, one of the leaders. Each had a name tag in bold red color that was impossible to miss. Paul had gotten her up to speed about Reed and vice versa and what she would be doing to help out.

"So good to meet you, Nikki," he beamed. "It's a pity that Trish couldn't be here to see what she made happen."

"She'll hear about it when she wakes up," Nikki told him optimistically.

"That's the spirit." Reed smiled, and the wrinkles at his eyes creased. "I hope you're ready to man the dunk tank. And there are many contestants in that raffle."

"I hope I'm up for it," Nikki replied and turned to

check out the surroundings. "It seems we're going to get a good crowd."

"We usually do at this time of year," Reed said as he came up to her, his hands shoved into the pocket of his jeans. "With so many seasonal things here on the island, people look forward to the summer festivities. Believe me when I say you'll have your hands full."

"I have no doubt about it. This place is all too familiar for me," Nikki replied.

"Trish used to say that all the time too," Reed muttered, and when Nikki looked over at him, she could see the sadness in his eyes. He missed her. "I'm having a hard time doing all of this without her. We are, I mean," he said, motioning to the man and woman behind him busy handing out pamphlets about recycling and protecting the coral reef.

"I know," Nikki told him. "We just have to have faith that she'll pull through."

"She will." He smiled. "She's as tough as nails."

She could see his admiration for Trish, and her heart warmed that she had been surrounded by so many great people. It only made her hope even more for her recovery.

"Okay," Reed said, rubbing his hands together. "I think it's time for a little fun."

It was early afternoon, and the patrons kept pouring in. A slight wind countered the sun's heat, and Nikki was grateful for it. She passed by the bingo table to see that Ava was having fun. She ruffled her hair and kept going.

She climbed the steps to the large, portable pool and picked up the megaphone. She had never done that sort of thing before, but she was feeling excited. Maybe it was contagious because the air was buzzing with it.

"Ladies and gentlemen, boys and girls!" she called over the loudspeaker. "Are you ready to have some fun?!"

"Woo-hoo! Yay!" they screamed.

"All right then." Nikki laughed. "How about we start by getting these officers wet!"

"Oh yeah!" a woman close by screamed.

"That's your cue, boys," she told the group of men who'd already stripped down to their swimming trunks. "You know the drill. Who's first to take the hot seat?"

Everyone hollered and hooted as one of the officers stepped forward. "Okay, let's get this over with. It's a hot day anyway."

"That's the spirit," Nikki said as she held up the officer's hand. "Now, let's see who's got an arm strong enough to take this man down!"

One by one, the men standing around the pool took their shot at the lever. Some of the balls barely tipped the seat, and the officer gripped the sides to keep from falling. When a large, heavyweight man stepped forward, he knew he was done for. The crowd cheered hard and loudly as the first officer hit the water with a great splash.

It continued in the same way until it was the police chief's turn. "Do I really have to?" he asked as he stood next to the hot seat.

"Do you even have to ask?" Nikki goaded him.

"Get on the seat!" someone shouted.

"I hate to agree, Chief," Nikki told him. "You have to take the seat, or I'm going to have to make you."

"How do you plan on doing that?" the chief asked as he stood with his hands on his hips.

"Should I show him?" Nikki asked the jeering crowd.

"Yeah!" they hollered back.

"Alright," she said as the chief looked at her suspiciously. She inched a little closer.

"Hey, what are you doing?" he asked and stepped back.

"Nothing," she said as she lunged forward and tapped him on the chest. He tipped backward, and his arms flailed as he tried to grab something to hold. The crowd celebrated as they watched his inevitable fall, and Nikki unwittingly got too close.

She shrieked when he caught her arm, and she managed at the last minute to ditch the megaphone as both she and the police chief hit the water, much to the amusement of everyone.

Nikki bobbed to the top and wiped her hand down her face as the chief joined her, laughing uproariously. "You didn't think I was going to take the fall alone, did you?"

Nikki laughed as some of the other men helped her out of the tank, but it was a rousing way to start the games and shenanigans.

The food was great, and she visited a couple of the tables for games before the evening rolled around and it was time for the raffle. The prize was one thousand dollars and some small appliances for runners-up.

Nikki called the winning numbers to an attentive group of people, and cheers erupted when the winners came to collect their prizes. It was an eventful day, and by the end of it, Nikki was exhausted.

She was making her way to one of the kiosks to get a drink when she ran into Paul and a beautiful young woman. "Nikki," he exclaimed. "You did such a great job out there."

"Tell that to my wet clothes." She laughed. "Ava had

to get me a change of outfit."

The young woman laughed. "It looked like fun, though."

"Oh, this is Sarah, my daughter, and her fiancé, Aaron," Paul said as he introduced them.

"Oh," Nikki replied with surprise. "She's beautiful, Paul. Nice to meet you both."

Sarah blushed. "I've heard about you." She nudged her very embarrassed father.

"Babe, maybe we can go and get a drink," Sarah suggested to Aaron and pulled him away from them.

"Is she...?" Nikki asked with amusement and pointed at the hastily departing couple.

"Yep," Paul said in answer to her unfinished question. "Trying to play cupid."

Nikki laughed. "Kids."

"Not so much these days," Paul replied. "Now she's off to get married."

Nikki got quiet as she thought about the child she never got to have. Paul must have noticed, and she blushed when she realized he was looking intensely at her.

"The private investigator came to the restaurant yesterday. Maybe we can meet up tomorrow and talk about how we'll handle the news about Amy."

"So you do know something," Nikki said.

"I never said I didn't, but I didn't have all the information. I still don't. Not until I meet with him. But what I do know is that she has been trying to find her daughter for months. Maybe longer. She was very anxious about meeting her and what it would be like."

"I can't say I don't know what that feels like." Nikki started feeling nervous all over again. "I'm curious to know more about her. What if she doesn't want to come here, like Trish thought? Trish only mentioned that if I didn't want a stake in the Nestled Inn I could sell it to Amy. But what if Amy doesn't want it or anything to do with either of us?"

She remembered what Ava had told her before but couldn't help feeling doubtful again.

"Don't worry about that now. I would suspect that the inn would fall to you if that's the case, but let's wait until we get to that bridge, okay?"

"Yeah, you're right," she told him. "Listen, I had a long day. I need to get back and wash off some of this sweat and dust."

Paul laughed. "Okay. We'll catch up."

She walked away, and before she could get to Ava, a middle-aged woman approached her. "You're Trish's sister, right?" she asked.

Her dark eyes flashed with concern at Nikki. "Yes, I'm Nikki."

She took Nikki's hands in hers. "She's in our prayers. She's a wonderful woman, and I know she'll pull through."

Nikki choked back the tears as the woman expressed her heartfelt sympathy regarding Trish. "Thank you."

It was the same as she continued to where Ava was. Several of the townspeople encouraged her and expressed their sympathies. It was a very emotional evening, and though a very entertaining day, she was glad it was over.

She met up with Ava, and they left, but as they pulled out of the parking lot, she saw Paul standing a little way off, watching her leave.

And for a moment, she thought there might still be something between them.

Chapter Seven

It was a bittersweet day that followed.

Nikki got up to see Ava packing her things, and her face fell. "I can't believe it's already been a week, and you're leaving."

She walked over and rested her head on Ava's shoulder.

"Oh, I know, but work calls," she said sorrowfully. "I wish I could stay longer."

"You can just quit your job and move here," Nikki teased.

"After you." Ava laughed, reminding her that she didn't live there either. "But you're in good hands. I see I have nothing to worry about with Paul around."

"Not really," Nikki said wistfully. "He's been a real angel. I don't know how I'd have managed all along if he wasn't around."

"I still think there's a future for the two of you," Ava added playfully as she zipped up her carry-on.

"Not going there with you." Nikki walked off to the kitchen, where she poured a cup of coffee. "Paul and I are just friends, and that's the way it's going to be. Now, how about we have brunch before you leave?"

"You're always so good at changing the subject." Ava shook her head.

"That's why I'm a journalist." Nikki grinned.

Ava rolled her eyes. "I'm going to wash up."

"Okay," she said.

The two lounged around the house all morning until it was time for brunch. "I can't tell you how I'm going to miss the food here," Ava said as they left the house and walked over to the Nestled Inn.

They ran into Dorothy as she wheeled the cart toward the elevator. "Hi, Dorothy."

"Hello, ma'am." She smiled and wiped her hand down the front of her apron. "I was just heading over to see if you needed any help with the housekeeping. Is now a good time?"

"Yes, Dorothy. We were just heading to brunch," Nikki replied.

"Very well." She smiled. "Enjoy."

"Thanks, Dor," Nikki said affectionately. Although she was just a staff member, Dorothy had been more like family to her since she'd been there.

The women entered the restaurant attached to the inn and found two other couples. She smiled and waved at them as she tried to maintain the family ambience Trish had obviously cultivated.

"I'm going to miss it here." Ava sighed. "It really feels like a slice of heaven."

"And here's to your send-off," Nikki said as Justin, one of the servers, brought a bottle of wine over to them.

Nikki had barely inherited the place, but it already felt like home to her. Not long after the wine, they enjoyed french onion soup with baguettes, followed by a rack of lamb with braised asparagus and squid-ink rice.

"I've never had this," Ava said of the rice. "It's very delicious."

"Me neither, and so many other things Paul has introduced me to since I've been there. I can't say my budget has ever allowed for frequent visits to Michelin-starred restaurants."

"You can say that again," Ava said as she cut into her lamb. "This is so juicy and tender it just melts in your mouth. How do they get it so soft?"

"Well, you're not going to understand because you're no cook," Nikki teased.

"Hey, I cook," Ava replied, feigning insult. "I cook a mean omelet, and my baked mac and cheese is to die for."

"Ava, making it from the box and sticking it into the oven isn't baked mac and cheese." Nikki laughed.

"Fine!" Ava pouted. "But that's why I'm friends with you. And now Paul."

Nikki laughed. "Yep. Give me a second, will you? Do you need more wine?"

"No, I'm good with this," Ava replied.

Nikki had to do some last-minute checks as she entered the kitchen to take stock of her inventory. Luckily, she was a foodie, so she knew about food pairings and how to sanitize a workstation.

"All good in here?" she asked Doug, the head chef.

"All good." He smiled back. "How did you like that lamb?"

"It was perfect," Nikki beamed. "Excellent service as always. Do you need anything? I'm going to head out for a few."

He looked around. "Maybe some fresh herbs, dry rub, but that's pretty much it."

"Okay," Nikki told him. "Keep up the good work," she called to the rest of the staff as she walked out.

Kaylyn was by the front when she left, and she waved goodbye to them.

"How is this work?" Ava asked with a laugh as they got to the car. "This is just being paid for having fun and relaxing. Do you think maybe you can hire me?"

Nikki laughed. "Just get out of here, will you?"

"I'll call you when I get home," Ava said as the two hugged.

Nikki watched her leave, and sadness quickly descended upon her. She would miss the late-night conversations, the teasing, and the support Ava offered.

Her spirit was low when she returned to the house, and she walked aimlessly into the bedroom. She didn't know much about her sister, and it seemed the whole town knew more than she did.

There must be pictures of her or keepsakes that could draw them closer. Nikki felt like a fake in her own sister's home.

She sat on the edge of the bed, wondering where Trish would keep her personal belongings, when her eyes caught on the closet. She'd watched enough movies to know there was always a shoebox of things or a chest in the attic. Since there was no attic or basement, her best bet was a possible shoebox.

She got up and opened the closet door, and sure enough, she found a couple of shoeboxes. She was reaching for one of them when she knocked them all over, and she jumped back as the contents spilled onto the floor.

"Shoot!" she said as she crouched on the ground next to them. She wasn't sure what belonged where, and she didn't want Trish to know she was messing with her things.

But then a picture of the entire family caught her eye. She sat on the floor and looked at it. They were on the boat. This time on the neighboring Whidbey Island, and Nikki's eyes watered as she remembered a time when they were together and happy.

There were several other pictures of family gatherings, school plays, and games that they went to. She covered her mouth as the memories washed over her. She was still going over the pictures when she spotted a folded manila envelope. She checked the contents and saw that it was documentation about the adoption.

It seemed Trish had been trying to find Amy for a long time, and Nikki felt a tug on her heart as she finally understood. If Trish had given Amy to her, she would have never really been her daughter. There would have come a time when Trish would have wanted her daughter back.

She rifled through the other papers when she saw an envelope with her name on it. Her heart thudded as she opened it and read what she recognized as Trish's handwriting.

Dearest Nikki,

I'm so sorry for all the pain I caused you so many years ago. I didn't really

understand what it was like for you back then, not being able to have a child.

I guess you could say I was selfish. Looking back, I regret what I did. I could have been assured that my daughter had a safe and loving home with you.

Instead, I robbed us both of time with her, and I caused you a lot of pain, and for

that, I am deeply sorry. I'm not sure we'll ever see each other again. It's become

too hard it seems, but I hope we will. I've missed you, and I love you with all my

heart...

Nikki couldn't hold back the tears as she rocked on her heels and stared at the paper. They'd only seen each other at their parents' funeral, and although living only an hour away, it hadn't drawn them closer.

Nikki felt like the guiltier party since she was the one who walked away. Trish had just been waiting for her to make the next move, and she never had. Nikki would have still been in Arlington if Trish hadn't been in the accident, and she felt ashamed.

The letter went on to say that she'd found her daughter, and though she was terrified that she might reject her, she still had to meet her.

Nikki was beside herself with emotion when someone knocked on the door. She looked around at the scattered paper on the ground. She started shoveling them together with her hands and putting them in the boxes. She was sure she was getting it wrong, but she couldn't just leave them there for others to see.

She eventually managed to open the door just as Kaylyn was about to walk away. "Oh, I didn't realize you were here. What's wrong?" she asked when she noticed Nikki's tearstained face.

"Nothing," Nikki replied, not wanting to be vulnerable in front of Kaylyn. "Why did you come by?"

"Nonsense," the woman said as she ushered Nikki into the room. "You can talk to me. Is it Trish? Did you get bad news?"

"No," Nikki said hurriedly. "Nothing's changed."

"Well," Kaylyn said and steered her to the sofa. "Trish and I were very good friends, almost like sisters, and she used to confide in me about everything."

"Everything?" Nikki asked reluctantly. "Even about me?"

"Yes. How did you think I recognized you when you walked in? It was as if I knew you too, so don't be shy. Just tell me what has made you so worked up."

She sat patiently, waiting for Nikki to gather her bearings. "I was just feeling guilty that I seem to be the only one who doesn't know who my sister is, and that's no one's fault but mine. I found a letter that she wrote to me apologizing..." Nikki said and started to cry again. "I was such an awful sister."

"Oh, don't say that," Kaylyn said and hugged her. "You were both very young and confused, but she never harbored any grudges against you. And she always loved you."

"I've always loved her." Nikki sobbed. "But I was wrong, and now I might lose her and never get the chance to tell her how sorry I am."

"No, don't think like that," Kaylyn said as she rocked her like a mother would her child. "She'll be fine, and so will you, okay?"

Nikki nodded just before she pulled back and wiped her eyes. "Why are you here?"

"I was just coming to check in on you and to tell you we're fully booked. We may need to get some more supplies as well because we're running low on cleaning items."

"Okay, I'll see about that right away." Nikki smiled. "Thanks for being a good friend."

"No problem," Kaylyn said and got up.

Nikki felt a little better after Kaylyn left, but not completely. It was hard for her to gather the remaining items for the shoeboxes.

That evening, she went to visit Trish. She lay as before, with her eyes closed and needles poking out of her arms, giving her sustenance and life.

She squeezed her hand. "I hope you can hear me, Trish, but I need you to come back. Please fight! I have a lot that I want to say to your face, like how sorry I am for being such an idiot for so long. And I will keep coming here every day until you wake up. You hear me! You know how stubborn I can be!"

She sighed as she looked at the still figure before her, but for the first time, she actually felt like she'd heard her.

She rose and kissed her bandaged forehead moments before she pulled back and noticed the single tear that escaped Trish's eye.

Chapter Eight

He wasn't sure why he was so anxious to meet Nikki at the pub. Maybe because it felt like an actual date.

He got there first and ordered a glass of whiskey from the bar so he could calm his nerves. He was also anxious about the information in the folder he carried. It was heavy, all the things he'd found out, and he hoped Nikki was up for the task.

A smile spread across his face when he noticed her arrival. She wore black leatherette leggings with a single-shoulder moss-green top. Her large, loose curls fell to her shoulders and bounced as she walked. He waved to her, and she smiled as she hurried over to him.

"I'm not late, am I?" she asked innocently.

"Now, why does that question sound so familiar?" he teased as Nikki blushed.

"I don't know." She laughed.

"Some things never change," he said.

The pub was dimly lit at the oval bar, where a few men drank and laughed heartily. There was a section where others congregated for live music and the dining area to the left.

"This is a really nice spot," she said as she looked around at the impeccable dining area with the rustic wooden tables and furnishings. Off-white table linens adorned the tables set with silver cutlery and had the wineglasses turned upside down.

The easy rhythm of blues played in the background, and he could tell she was already enjoying herself.

"Outside of Lot 28, this is where I go," he commented.

"I bet most people do." Nikki smiled. "Not everyone can afford lobster bisque and squid-ink pasta," she joked.

He laughed. "Yeah, you're probably right. They have great finger food here," he said as he showed her the menu. "Care to have a look?"

"Don't mind if I do," she said as she scanned the menu card. "Tacos sound good, and chicken lollipops."

"I agree." He grinned. "You took the words right out of my mouth."

She laughed as he placed the order. He couldn't deny that he enjoyed her company, and though he hadn't thought about her in years, lately, he'd found that she was always on his mind.

But that wasn't why they'd met. They enjoyed the meal, somewhat anxiously as they both knew why they had met in the first place.

When they were done eating, they retreated to a lounge area to talk. He could see how nervous she was. "Are you ready?" he asked.

She sighed. "Before you do that, I know how close you and Trish are, but how much do you know? I can't help but think that if she told you about Amy, then you must know a lot about us too."

"You don't have to feel bad about anything, Nikki," he told her. "I already knew you and your family long before Trish and I ran into each other. Maybe that was why she found it so easy to talk to me."

"I think I'm going to need another glass of wine," Nikki lamented, much to his amusement.

He signaled the server over, who promptly returned with a bottle of red wine. Nikki held the glass in her hand very timidly as she glanced over at Paul. "Do you know what happened all those years ago?"

He nodded his head. "Yeah, she told me about it," he admitted. "She told me how she'd gotten pregnant with this guy who ditched her afterward, and that when her parents found out, they pressured her into leaving Seattle for Arlington, where she would put the baby up for adoption." Paul took her hand. "Nikki, you have to understand that Trish didn't want to give you her daughter because she had every intention of getting her back. She wasn't out to hurt you."

"What?" Nikki asked and raised her brows.

"That's why she started trying to find Amy. Ever since she's been here, she's been looking, but it's a lot harder than it seems."

"Wait," Nikki said and wrinkled her face. "Trish wanted to keep the baby back then?"

"She did, but her father threatened to cut her off if she didn't give her up for adoption, and your mother couldn't disagree with him," Paul told her and sighed.

"I didn't know that. She told me no right off the bat, so I thought it was her decision too," Nikki said softly.

"No, there was an entire conversation that happened

before you showed up," he said. "She's harbored the guilt of that moment for years. She's never forgiven herself, and that's why she wants to connect with Amy, especially because she hasn't had any other children after that."

He could see the pain written across Nikki's face. "I'm not telling you any of this so you can feel guilty, Nikki," he reassured her. "I just want you to understand, and so does Trish, that none of this can be blamed on either of you."

"I see," Nikki said as she toyed with her fingers. "What's Amy like?" she asked.

He slid the folder across the table. "Have a look," he said.

Nikki picked up the file like she expected it could break between her fingers, and a smile spread across her face when she saw Amy's picture. "She looks like Trish," she said lovingly. "Did she have a good life?"

"Yeah, for the most part," Paul replied.

Nikki sighed and closed the file. "That's more than can be said of me and Trish," she replied.

"I have to admit Trish didn't go that far back," Paul said. "I mean, you and I dated for a while, but I wasn't at your house all the time."

"I know, and you wouldn't have wanted to be," she said. "My father was a workaholic and a perfectionist. He rolled in the big leagues, and because of his reputation, he was sort of famous too. And he guarded that with his life."

Paul tapped the folder. "I can see that. Trish had mentioned that he didn't want her having a baby as a teenager to tarnish his reputation."

"Yep," Nikki said sadly. "That was all he cared about. Not her. Not me, and certainly not Mom. He had to look good all the time, and we were often ushered into the shadows. We had to become journalists like him. Even in that, we didn't have a choice."

"You didn't want to be a journalist?" Paul asked as his brows dipped.

"I did, but if I hadn't, he'd have forced the issue. For a while, Trish didn't want to do that," Nikki told him. "But he told her she had to have the baby and then come back to Seattle University to study journalism, and she did. But as you can see, she wanted to run a business."

"Life wasn't all roses and unicorns," Paul replied. "I can't say there was much difference in my own household. Not my parents, I mean," he said as he explained and crossed his arms on the table.

"With your wife and daughter, you mean?" Nikki asked sensitively.

"Yeah." He sighed as he stared at the table. "It's been ten years, and the wound still feels fresh. It was a jarring time when I found out she had late-stage leukemia. Sarah was only thirteen when we found out, and that took a turn for the worst," he said.

"I can't imagine it was easy for you to handle a teen girl," Nikki said.

"You have no idea," he replied. "After Nat died, it was even worse. I was hurting, and there were times I had to just lock away what I was feeling to try to deal with what Sarah was going through."

"As if the teenage years weren't bad enough," Nikki said with understanding. "I'm sorry you had to go through that all alone. It was clearly not easy. I remember what it was like losing my parents, and I wasn't even close to them at the time. But they're your parents, you know?"

"Yeah," Paul said and wiped his hands down the

corners of his mouth. "Why is there so much sadness between us?"

Nikki laughed softly. "I don't know," she replied. "Bad luck?"

"Perhaps," Paul replied. "How about livelier things. You are a big-shot journalist like your father."

She smiled. "Yeah, I've been killing it for the past twenty years at the *Providence Journal*."

"Picked up where your dad left off?"

"Something like that," she said. "I love doing it, but my ex-husband hated it. He thought I should have done something more 'respectable' like report on war crimes."

"He clearly didn't know you well," Paul replied. "You? In a war zone?"

Nikki laughed. "You know me all too well. I like safety."

"As we all should," he said and started to stare at her until he could see the discomfort on her face. "I don't mean to make you uncomfortable, but it's hard not to wonder, why now? Why are you back now?"

"Paul, I try not to get too serendipitous when it comes to us. I don't want to get ahead of anything and then get disappointed. I just want to focus on my sister for now."

"I know," he said as he reached for the file again. "Where do you want us to begin?"

"We know she lives in Seattle, which is great. That's close by versus if she were living in New York now or Alaska."

"True," Nikki replied.

"She's a server, by what's in here. She's had some run-ins with some bad company and has trouble with an ex-boyfriend or boyfriend," he said as he lifted his head to look at her. "How do you want to approach her?"

"I mean, it's very convenient that she works as a server," Nikki told him. "We could go to Seattle to the restaurant where she works. Keep an eye on her for a night or two and see what she's like."

Paul knitted his brows. "You're not trying to delay the inevitable, are you?"

"No, no," Nikki assured. "I just don't think I'd want some strangers showing up out of the blue to tell me that I'm their long-lost aunt and I'm adopted."

"Hmm," he mused. "You may have a point. But won't she get suspicious if she sees us there all the time and *then* we tell her who we are? Maybe a direct approach is better."

"The two ways have their merits," Nikki agreed. "Okay, here's what we can do. How about we go there and just go with the flow? Maybe we'll say it on day one, or we'll wait."

"I can live with that. When do you want to go?" he asked.

"As soon as possible. We've waited long enough, and I'm afraid I might get cold feet if we keep dragging this out."

"I don't think that's going to be a problem." Paul smiled.

"Besides, I want to make sure that when Trish wakes up, her daughter will possibly be by her side. She might be disappointed if we haven't reached out to her yet."

"You're right. Weekends are busier, so how about we go this Friday evening, and maybe we tell her then or wait until Saturday?"

"Sounds like a plan." Nikki smiled and finally relaxed into the chair.

She wasn't the only anxious one. He'd seen how

71

much it had eaten away at Trish because she couldn't accept that she'd given up her child. Now, looking at Nikki, he couldn't help but think that the three made an odd group—all having lost loves and parents who died.

Maybe it made them uniquely suited for each other, but he didn't want to read too much into it either.

He would go where the wind took him, but not if he wasn't the one guiding the sails. He'd had enough pain and disappointment.

He could do without one more.

Chapter Nine

Nikki settled into her role as part-time manager and proprietor at the Nestled Inn.

The staff had already warmed to her, and during the two and a half weeks she'd been there, she'd been invited to dinner and several brunches.

Kaylyn had become a close friend of hers in the absence of Ava, and she relied on her guidance and support, considering she was more familiar with the business end.

Nikki stood at the front desk with Kaylyn one morning when Kaylyn nudged her. She turned to look at the woman, wondering why she was poking her when she saw the look on her face and where she was looking.

Nikki looked up at the door and saw Reed Story walk into the inn. He was casually dressed in a pair of jeans, a button-down, and loafers. He wore a marine cut, and his face was clean-shaven.

"What's wrong?" Nikki asked Kaylyn. She'd seen Reed before, the first time being when she was hosting the last fundraiser, so she wasn't sure what Kaylyn wanted to tell her.

She didn't get a chance to talk before he approached the front desk. "Hello," he said with a broad smile. "Can we talk?"

Nikki looked over at Kaylyn, and then back at Reed. She wondered if the woman knew something she didn't. "Sure," she said and stepped around the desk. "Maybe we can go out to the patio."

"Great," he said and ushered her in front of him.

Nikki didn't know what the meeting was about, and all sorts of ideas started floating around in her head. She was nervous as she sat across from Reed and folded her hands in her lap.

"While I'm here, maybe we should get something to eat," he suggested.

Nikki wasn't hungry, but she knew it would be rude to refuse, so she accepted. They ordered from the lunch menu, which consisted of sandwiches and finger foods, and she nibbled on them while they engaged in small talk.

She knew he was still waiting to broach the real subject and tried to be patient.

"I have to admit, I'm very curious about what we're doing out here," she finally said. "Is it something about the Humane Society? Because I'm more than willing to take my sister's place in whatever she used to do before."

Reed laughed. "I don't know how much you've realized since you've been here, but Trish was sort of...special to me." He eyed Nikki.

It was then she understood Kaylyn's nudging, and she was instantly relieved. "Are you two involved?" she asked pointedly.

"Not so much, but I have taken an interest in her. Our

time was cut short after the accident, but I'm holding on to the hope that she will recover."

Nikki was floored by the romanticism he was expressing. He was willing to wait for her comatose sister to regain consciousness so he could continue to pursue her.

"Oh, that's so sweet," Nikki gushed and locked her fingers beneath her chin.

Reed blushed a little and cleared his throat. "Needless to say, she has been very instrumental in many of the Humane Society's activities."

"I can see that," Nikki said as she remembered her episode with the dunk tank.

"She has helped me raise money for the animal shelter, the children's hospital, the food bank, and so many other events throughout the community."

Nikki listened to him talking about Trish, and she could hear the admiration seeping out of the man. "She seems to have been loved by all."

"She is," he said quickly. "A couple of us were talking, especially after the last fundraiser she planned, and we would like to return the favor."

Nikki's brows dipped. "I'm not following."

"She has helped so many of us that now we want to help her," he added.

"How?" Nikki couldn't imagine they could do anything for Trish other than pray for her and visit with her.

"We were thinking that we can host an event right here where everyone comes together, and we pray for her recovery. That is if it's alright with you. You're the boss now." He smiled.

Tears welled up in Nikki's eyes. "Are you kidding me? Of course, you can do that. Why would I object?"

He rubbed his palms together with glee. "I know you wouldn't say no, but I had to ask."

Nikki had thought he had feelings for Trish, but it was apparent that it ran a lot deeper than a superficial liking. He might even be in love with her, and she wondered how long he'd been keeping it to himself.

"When do you want to do this?" Nikki asked anxiously. "I'm already excited. And what did you have in mind?"

"Well," he began, "we were thinking about a get-together where the entire community comes together, sort of like a game evening, and we can share things about Trish that we like. Perhaps we can fundraise to help with the medical bills and then end with praying. What do you think?"

"That sounds great, Reed," Nikki said. "I'm all in. Let's do this." She wiped the tears of joy that flowed from her.

"Now, don't think you have to do much," he told her matter-of-factly. "My team and I will do everything—the music, the chairs and tables, the schedule, the drinks, and the like. What I would want from you is finger foods because this is Lot 28, after all." He chuckled. "Nobody does it better than you."

"You've got it. Just name it and when."

"How about this weekend?" he asked. "I know that doesn't give us a lot of time, but we have almost everything we need. We do this so often it's like having dinner at home." He leaned forward and said with great familiarity.

"Maybe next weekend will be better. I have to go out of town this weekend. Plus, it would give you some more time to advertise it."

"Sounds like a plan." He grinned.

She could see how much he was beaming that he was able to do something for Trish other than sitting around and waiting for her to wake up. She knew the feeling well, and she was all for it.

Reed left shortly after that, and Nikki returned inside feeling like she was floating on air. Kaylyn called her over.

"What was that about?" she asked eagerly.

"He wants to host an event here in honor of Trish," she said excitedly. "Like a games evening, fundraiser, and prayer event all rolled into one."

Kaylyn slapped her hand to her mouth. "Are you kidding me? That's great. When?"

"Next weekend," Nikki replied.

"Oh," Kaylyn said as a worried look came over her face. "Will we have everything ready in time for that? I need to go check..."

"Oh no." Nikki stopped her. "He said we don't have to do anything other than provide finger food. He's got it all under control."

"I knew he had a good heart," Kaylyn beamed. "And I always suspected he had a sweet spot for Trish. He was always coming around. When he came in, I thought he was growing sweet on you too."

Nikki laughed. "That's what that poking was about."

Kaylyn giggled and blushed. "I'm glad to see that I was wrong."

"Yes, you were, and that makes two of us, by the way," she replied. "I'm still not sure if I'll be here long-term."

Kaylyn waved her off. "If you get to a month, you're officially a resident." She laughed.

Nikki smiled at her suggestion as well, but if she were there for a month, it could be assumed that Trish would be in a coma for as long, and she couldn't imagine her sister sleeping for a prolonged period while the world continued around her.

"I still think we need to prep the staff so they know what to expect, just in case they need something," Kaylyn said.

"That's a good idea. I'll call a meeting to alert them and decide what finger foods to provide."

The women separated, and Nikki was heading to the house when she spotted an elderly woman sitting in the back, eyeing her. She lifted her feeble arms and motioned to Nikki.

She had never seen her before, so she wondered if she needed help. "Hi," she said when she made it to the table. "Do you need help? Did you place an order?"

"No." The woman chuckled and motioned to her to sit. "You're the older sister, right?"

Nikki sat across from the woman. She seemed vaguely familiar, but she'd spent so much time in Camano as a child that she'd probably met her years ago before she'd hightailed it out of town.

"I am," she said as she searched her memory. "I'm sorry, have we met? I've met so many people since I came here."

"Not this time." She smiled. "I just wanted to come and see you. I've seen Trish a couple of times, and she visits with me when she can, but I was friends with your parents."

"Oh," Nikki said in shock. "How did you know them?"

"I was very good friends with them." She smiled.

Nikki couldn't say she could agree with or refute the claims. Her parents didn't always entertain their friends at the house, plus she wouldn't have been of the mind to take note of her parents' friends.

"Well, it's good to meet you," Nikki said and took the wrinkled hand the woman proffered. "I wish we were meeting on better terms."

"Ah," she said and waved her off. "Any terms are good terms is what I always say." She smiled.

"You may have a point there," Nikki said. "Do you live here on Camano Island?"

"Yes," the woman replied. "That's how I met your parents when you all used to come here as children during the summer. You came to my house once or twice, but that was about it. I didn't expect either of you to remember me. Plus, I looked a whole lot better." She laughed. "I'm Nelly, by the way. I forgot to say."

Nikki laughed. She could tell she was going to like the woman. "It's a pleasure meeting you, Nelly. I don't know how long I'll be here, but if you need anything, you know where to find me."

"That's awfully kind of you, dear." She smiled. "You're every bit as sweet as your sister. Just know I'm praying for her."

"Thank you," Nikki said as her resident lump returned to her throat. "Oh, speaking of which, the Humane Society will be hosting an event for her next weekend. I hope you can make it."

"Oh, I didn't know that," she said as she tried to remember.

"No, it isn't public knowledge yet," Nikki said before the lines on her forehead smoothed over. "Reed and I just agreed on it. It's short notice, so I hope we can get the word out fast enough."

"Well, I'll be there," Nelly promised.

"I'm happy to hear it. Would you like something to eat? Or drink?"

"Oh," she said as she struggled to stand. "There's very little I can eat these days without needing a pill for this or an injection for that," she said. "Make sure you treat your body right," she warned Nikki, who helped her get to her feet. "When you're older, everything breaks easily, but it all starts breaking when you're young."

"That's pretty good advice," Nikki replied.

"I'll see you around." She smiled at Nikki, and her gray eyes twinkled.

Nikki's heart warmed as she watched the woman leaving. She'd never known grandparents, but something told her that Nelly just might be that kind of woman.

It would seem her life had been revamped since her arrival in Camano, and as she walked back to the house, she wondered if her stay might not be permanent after all.

Chapter Ten

Nikki woke up in a cold sweat.

At first, she couldn't quite put her finger on why until she leaned across and picked up her phone to check for messages. That was when she saw one from Paul:

What time do you want us to come over?

Her eyes widened, and her heart started racing. They were supposed to meet with the private investigator. Once more, feelings of paranoia, excitement, and anxiety overwhelmed her, and she slipped from the bed to wash up.

She splashed cold water onto her face and smoothed her hair back with her damp palms. It didn't matter how she felt—she wanted to meet Amy, and it was—is—what Trish wanted her to do.

She returned to the bedroom and replied to Paul before she made a beeline for the closet to pick out something decent enough for a visitor.

It was already nine, so she had roughly an hour to get ready. She was sitting by the kitchen island, clutching her coffee mug nervously between her palms when the doorbell rang.

This is it!

"Hello," she said as she pulled the door in. "Come in."

"Hello," the gentleman replied and walked by her.

She smiled up at Paul and followed the man, allowing him to close the door. The private investigator looked just as she imagined he would—military-cut hair, clean-shaven face, and a sturdy gait. He was dressed in a pair of jeans, a white polo shirt, and loafers—very textbook, but he had a kind and gentle demeanor as he turned to face her with an extended hand.

"I'm so sorry about your sister," he said.

Nikki took his hand. "Thank you. I have no doubt she'll dodge this. She's very good at making narrow escapes."

The man smiled broadly. "I hope you're right." His eyes shifted to Paul, and he lifted the large manila envelope he carried. "I don't mean to be hasty, but I have another appointment in an hour."

"Oh yeah, no problem," Nikki replied, showing him to the living room. "Please, have a seat. Would you like anything? Coffee? Water? Juice?"

"If it were another time, I'd ask for chicken parm, but not now," he said as he made a crack at Paul.

Paul laughed. "Anytime, Greg. What do you have?"

He rubbed his palms and motioned for Nikki to join him. She felt like her heart was creeping up her throat, and when she sat next to Paul, she could barely breathe.

Greg was very deliberate in his motions, it seemed to her—it took far too long to take a couple of pictures and a few sheets of paper from the envelope. But then, she wasn't sure if he was moving too slowly or her mind that was just going too fast. She sat gingerly on the edge of the seat; her hands clasped together.

She jumped when Paul reached out and took her hand. "It's okay," he told her.

She was relieved that she wasn't alone. Greg looked at them, his hands suspended in the air and gripping Nikki's heart at the same time.

He leaned forward and handed her a large picture. "This is Amy Foster."

Nikki's hands shook as she took the picture, and instantly, she clapped her hand over her mouth. Her eyes widened as she stared at the young girl looking back at her.

"Wow," Paul said over her shoulder. "She looks just like her."

"I guess it's safe to say then that we have the right person," Greg replied humorously.

Nikki laughed nervously. "You could say that," she said as she stared at Amy. Her hair was long and had ombre highlights. Her eyes were happy and kind. She seemed to have had a good life. "I can't wait to meet her," Nikki said listlessly.

"What else do you have?" Paul asked while Nikki continued to stare at the picture. Her eyes welled up with tears as she reflected on the fact that Trish had looked just like that when they had gotten into the fight.

"She was adopted by Bob and Linda Porter, and she lived with them in Seattle until she graduated from high school. Bob is a factory worker, and Linda worked at a daycare. Amy is currently living in an apartment with a roommate and working as a server."

"Already?" Nikki asked and knitted her brows. "She isn't in college?"

Greg sighed. "There's more," he said and pulled out another sheet of paper. "Over the years, Amy and some of their neighbors have called the police."

Nikki couldn't feel herself breathing. "Did he hit her?"

"It seems Bob is an alcoholic and would often get into a rage and strike Linda, but there's no mention here of hitting Amy," Greg said with a sigh.

Nikki was disheartened that Amy had grown up in an environment like that. "She must have been so unhappy," she mused. "No wonder she moved out as soon as she could."

Greg handed her another picture of a boy—he had dirty-blond hair that was spiked, a dragon tattoo on his neck, and a dangerous look in his eyes. He was the kind of cute, daring boy young girls would fall for, and Nikki dreaded what Greg was about to say next.

"That's Jake Tapper, Amy's on-and-off boyfriend," he said.

There it was.

"I hope she let him go," Nikki said, narrowing her eyes at the obvious playboy.

"From what I've gathered, they've broken up a couple of times, but it didn't stick."

Nikki instantly began to get concerned. She remembered how Trish had been left on her own when she'd gotten pregnant with Amy by a playboy. She didn't wish to see the same thing happen to her daughter.

Greg handed Nikki the envelope. "Everything else you might need is in there—addresses, friends, etc. Feel free to contact me if you need more information, but I think that should do it."

Paul instantly stood and held out his hand as Greg did the same. "It was a pleasure, man."

Greg smiled, nodded his head, and walked off toward the door. Nikki followed, carrying the picture of Amy still in her hand. She stared at the picture as she walked back to the living room and sighed as she sat.

"Still feeling nervous about meeting her?" Paul asked as he stood next to where she sat.

"I can't help it," she replied, and her hands dropped onto the seat. "She might not have had the best life growing up, but she seems to be doing okay now. What if we disrupt her life with this news? What if she doesn't even know she's adopted? We could ruin everything for her."

Paul sat next to her and took her hands in his. She stared at them for a couple of seconds before she raised her eyes to meet his. Instantly, an unfamiliar thought raced across her mind as she looked into kind eyes. *Why did she break up with him all those years ago?* She blinked rapidly to dispel the thoughts and cleared her throat.

"I know you're worried about all of this, but what if it makes her life easier to know? What if she already knows she's adopted?"

"I know, but when has life ever gone the way we wanted it to?" She sighed.

Paul chuckled. "I know, right? But this is what Trish wanted, and it's only fair that if Amy doesn't already know, she gets the chance to make up her own mind. You can't keep this from her."

"I know," Nikki replied.

"Look, it's not like you're going to be asking her to call it quits on her life and pack up her things and move. You're just going to tell her about her real mother. And her aunt. And that she was never 'given away.' She was always loved. That's it. The rest is up to her."

"Yeah, but now I'm also afraid of rejection," Nikki admitted. "This is the child I'd wanted. What if she doesn't want me now?"

"You won't know that until you give her the chance," Paul advised. "Just stop panicking. It's not doing any of us any good."

Nikki slipped her hand from Paul's hold and wiped them down her face. "I pray this works out the way it's supposed to." She cast her eyes upward to heaven. "At least once."

Paul chuckled. "Okay, I'll leave you alone to absorb this and get your head right. We leave on the weekend, so no freaking out before then."

She laughed. "I promise. Thanks, Paul. For everything."

"No sweat," he said and left.

Nikki knew she had to tell Trish about the discovery. She knew it would give her an additional reason to fight. As soon as Paul left, she was out the door too.

Her feelings of elation were instantly subdued when she walked into Trish's room and heard the constant beeping of the machines. She sighed as she pulled up the chair next to the bed—it had gotten harder with each visit to see her sister like that, but if she could really hear her, she didn't want her to be keen to the sadness in her voice.

She plastered a smile onto her face and took her hand. "I have good news for you. We found your daughter, Amy. Isn't that good news?" she asked and paused, like she was hoping for an answer, and wiped tears that spilled from the corners of her eyes. "She lives in Seattle and looks beautiful—just like you did when you were her age. I can't wait to meet her and for you to meet her when you wake up. You just need to promise to wake up. I've done my part. Now you need to do yours." She sniffled and stroked the back of Trish's hand. "We both need you."

Then she laid her head against Trish and closed her eyes as she prayed for a miracle.

Chapter Eleven

Nikki's hands shook as Paul pulled up outside of the restaurant. Her heart thumped in her chest, and her head ballooned.

"Maybe we're too early," she commented.

"It's happy hour," Paul told her. "We might be late."

"Oh dear." Nikki instantly pulled down the visor to use the mirror. She pinched her cheeks and smoothed her hair. "How do I look?"

"I doubt she will care about that," Paul replied.

"Humor me," Nikki insisted.

"You look fine," he told her. "Now, can we go before you get cold feet?"

Nikki placed her hands on her chest to help with steadying her wildly beating heart. "I feel like I'm going to pass out from anxiety."

"You're exaggerating," Paul replied and got out of the car. He met her by her door as she got out. She wore a pair of black skinny jeans and an airy white top that flowed over her hips. Ankle boots finished her look as she walked next to Paul who was similarly dressed in black jeans and a gray T-shirt.

The place was teeming with life when they walked in. It was either the hippest spot in Seattle or the only one.

"Isn't this a popular joint," Paul commented, echoing her thoughts.

"I was just thinking the same thing," Nikki said as they walked up to the desk. Luckily, they had a reservation. "Reservation for Humphry please," she told the obvious college student.

In fact, she wasn't the only one. The place was full of college students and otherwise young people. Music blared from the speakers, and the hum of voices filled the air.

"Right this way," the blond-haired attendant told them and led them to a table along the wall with the street view.

"Thank you," Nikki replied nervously as she took her seat. She instantly started looking around. "I wonder if she's already here."

"She should be," Paul noted. "Based on Greg's info, she starts her shift every evening at six."

"I don't see her," Nikki replied as she continued scanning the crowded vicinity for Amy. It was difficult for her to do with all the movement around them—servers and waitresses kept hurrying by, guests came and went, and it was a constant passing of bodies that her eyes felt like they'd pop out of her head.

"Just relax," Paul told her. "How about we get something to eat or drink to calm your nerves. If you meet her like that, you just might spook her."

Nikki's eyes widened as she looked at Paul. "You're right." She sucked in a deep breath, closed her eyes for a couple of seconds, and then opened them again. "Okay, I'm fine now." But moments later, her eyes were roaming again.

Paul laughed. "Don't worry. She's here," he said and chin-nodded past Nikki. "She's over at that table."

Nikki snapped her neck so fast that she almost got whiplash. "Where?" But she didn't have to look for too long. It was Amy. How could she miss seeing the face that looked just like the one she'd grown up with? "Oh my." She covered her mouth. "I thought she looked like Trish in the picture, but this is insane."

"Don't stare so hard," Paul warned. "You might creep out some folks."

Nikki tore her eyes away, but she had to force herself from looking back every couple of seconds. Her eyes followed her, as inconspicuous as she could, while she floated from table to table, wearing the same infectious smile. She wore the customary black-and-white outfit, and her hair was caught at her nape.

"I hope she comes to our table," Nikki said.

"Can you handle that?" Paul chuckled.

She'd hardly said the words when she noticed Amy coming toward them. "Oh shoot, she's coming."

Paul continued laughing at her. She was acting like a teenager, and Nikki knew it well, but she couldn't help it.

"Good evening," an all-too-familiar voice said as she stood next to the table. "I'm Amy, and I'll be your server for this evening. Are you ready to order, or do you need a couple of minutes?"

All Nikki could do was stare at her, which only produced tears. Amy started to look uncomfortable. "I'm sorry, what's wrong?"

"Nothing," Paul interjected. "She just got some news recently that still has her all worked up."

"Oh," Amy replied. "Should I come back?"

"I'm fine," Nikki replied instantly. She didn't want her to leave. "I'll have some lemon water."

"I'll have a Long Island iced tea," Paul said.

"I'll be right back." Amy hurried away.

"Oh God, I think I scared her off," Nikki said as guilt gripped her.

"Nah." Paul waved her off. "I'm sure she's seen worse customers." He grinned.

Nikki laughed. "Is that your way of making me feel better?"

"Depends if it's working or not."

"It's not," she groaned. "I feel like I'm about to sit for a bar exam."

"Whatever that feels like." Paul shrugged. "Just pull yourself together. Here she comes again."

Nikki sucked in a deep breath. She had every intention of not being weird, but she couldn't help but stare as Amy set the glasses down. "You're so beautiful," she blurted out.

Amy paused and stepped back a little. "What's the matter with you?" Paul hissed under his breath. "Forgive her," he told Amy, who seemed to be maintaining a safe distance. "I think we're ready to order. We'll just have the endless wings if you don't mind."

"I'll be right back with your order," Amy replied, scurrying off.

"Why are you trying to spook her off? You'll be lucky if she even comes back to this table," Paul accosted Nikki, though gently.

"I couldn't help it. It just slipped out," Nikki replied.

"If she does return, you need to keep a lid on it. You don't want to give her a bad impression of you only to turn around and tell her you're her long-lost aunt."

"You're right," Nikki replied, and then her eyes widened. "What if I've already ruined my chances?"

"Just try to relax," Paul implored her. "Let's just focus on what we came here to do and don't overthink it."

Nikki inhaled deeply. "I'll try." But it was easier said than done. Her eyes found Amy as she waited tables, and she forcibly kept quiet when she returned with their order. She wasn't hungry, so the wings tasted like paste in her mouth. She gave up after a while, but her roaming eyes kept searching for Amy.

Paul tried to distract her. "You do know we have to wait until the end of her shift to talk to her, right?"

"I know, but it's taking so long," she moaned, just as she noticed something off about Amy. She was waiting on a table at the back, but the guest seemed rude. She could see Amy's face visibly upset, and as soon as the man reached for her, she flinched and backed away. Other guests had begun to turn their heads to the man's raised voice, and a feeling of doom descended upon Nikki. She started to move.

Paul placed his hand on hers to keep her seated. "Are you crazy? You don't even know what's going on."

"It's not good," Nikki replied without taking her eyes off Amy. "He seems aggressive."

"It's not your place," Paul reminded her.

"She's my niece!" Nikki said louder than she had anticipated.

"She doesn't know that," he reminded her. "Here she comes again. Do nothing!"

Nikki ignored his warning. "Is everything alright?" Nikki asked her as soon as she got to the table.

Amy seemed dazed, and her color had faded. "Yeah, I'm fine," she said, immediately plastering a smile onto her face.

"I noticed that," Nikki said and thumbed toward the man.

"Oh, that," Amy replied with a casual laugh. "I get those customers all the time. Nothing new," she said and waved it off. "He was just upset about something on the menu."

Nikki didn't want to press it and scare Amy off even further, so she remained silent even though she still had a bad feeling in the pit of her stomach. She could barely see his face because of his positioning, but like Paul had said, there was nothing much she could do.

"Hey, do you have a minute after your shift ends? I'd like to speak to you for a moment," Nikki blurted out.

Amy narrowed her eyes at her. "Why?"

"There's something you need to know," Nikki told her flatly. "Please. I'll only take a few minutes of your time."

Amy's posture went rigid, and her eyes squinted. "Um, okay," she replied, almost reluctantly. "I'll meet you back here, then. My shift ends in an hour."

"Okay, and thanks." Nikki smiled. She shook when Amy walked off, and she looked across at Paul. "I feel like my insides are about to fall out."

Paul chuckled. "Well, this is an important moment. I'd be surprised if you weren't anxious at all."

The hour seemed to creep by. By the time Amy returned, she was practically a basket case. She pulled up a chair to the booth table they shared, all the while being careful not to sit too close to Nikki.

"Okay, what's this about?" Amy asked.

Nikki exhaled sharply. "I don't think there's any easy way to say this, so I'll just get on with it. I'm your aunt."

Amy looked confused. "Aunt? Mom doesn't have a sister."

"I'm your *real* mother's sister. Your biological mother," Nikki clarified. "Amy, you were adopted."

"Is this a prank or something?" she asked offensively as her features darkened.

"No, I swear, it's true," Nikki told her. "Your mother had to give you up because she was too young to take care of you."

"Why now?" Amy asked. "Twenty-one years, and *now* she's interested in me? She couldn't even come to face me herself?" Amy spat, and Nikki's worst fears began to materialize.

"She couldn't come," Nikki explained. "She was in a car accident and is in a coma now, but she was trying to find you before the accident. I came to finish what she'd started."

"I don't believe any of this nonsense," Amy said and pushed her chair back. "I have to go."

"Wait!" Nikki jumped up and handed Amy the envelope. "Here's proof. Everything about the adoption."

Amy stared at the envelope like it would swallow her up if she touched it. "That doesn't prove anything to me!" she snapped. "Is that the only reason you're here? To let me know that I was put up for adoption by a woman who is in a coma? What's the point of that? I find out I have another mother who's practically dead?"

Her words stung Nikki. "She's going to wake up, and she'll want to meet you."

"Too bad," Amy replied. "I don't want any part of this."

"Here," Nikki said quickly and handed her a card for the inn. "If you change your mind, this is where you can reach me. All my contact information is on it."

Amy stared at the card before she swiped it from Nikki's hand and brushed past her.

Paul got up and walked over to Nikki. He put his arm around her shoulders as they began to shake from her sobbing.

"I knew it!" she said through tears.

"Hey, you just shook her world with that bit of news. You didn't expect she'd be happy about it, did you?" He tried to console her. "Just give her some time to wrap her mind around it. I'm sure she'll reach out when she's ready."

Nikki wiped her eyes with the back of her hand. "You think so?"

"I know so," Paul replied. "Now, let's go. We've been here long enough."

Chapter Twelve

Nikki's feelings of despair did not dissipate quickly.

The following morning, she woke up feeling like she was the only person in the world and all hope was lost. Still, it felt like a dream.

She lay in bed and stared at the ceiling, hoping the patterned surface would bring her comfort or answers. She knew Amy wouldn't fall into her so easily, but she'd dreaded the rejection she'd received. It was Trish's wish for her to find her daughter, and while she'd accomplished that, she hadn't really brought her home. If Amy wanted nothing to do with them, she'd all but ruined Trish's chances of meeting her daughter.

She slipped from the bed and padded into the kitchen. The coffee machine had a timer, and the hot brew waited for her when she walked in. She loved the smell of freshly brewed coffee in the morning but couldn't appreciate it then.

She remembered what Paul had said to her—she just needed to give Amy some time. The problem was that she'd left a life back in Arlington indefinitely, and that period seemed to have been extended.

She poured the coffee and returned to the bedroom. Maybe Amy had already texted, she thought. Her heart started to race as she picked up the device, but there was no message from Amy. She noticed, however, a couple of missed calls from Ava.

She was about to put the phone down when it started ringing, and she jumped in fright. It was Ava, and though she wasn't in the mood for conversation, she needed a friend.

"Hey," she answered weakly.

"Okay, that's not the usual morning voice I get. What's wrong?"

"Nothing," Nikki lied, not because she wanted to, but simply because she didn't want to relive the last day.

"Um, I'm not sure who you think this is, but I know you better than that. So, spill it, and don't make me have to drive all the way to Camano Island to wring it out of you."

Nikki laughed softly. Ava was always good at lifting her spirits, which was one of the reasons she'd been her best friend for so many years. "Okay, fine," she relented. "I went to see Amy yesterday."

Ava squealed. "You found her? You must be so relieved. What's she like?"

"Does this sound like relief in my voice?" Nikki asked.

"Uh-oh, someone sounds mad," Ava replied, and Nikki could almost see her pouting lips.

"Sorry," she said and wiped her hand down her face. "It's just that it didn't go quite the way I wanted it to."

"What happened?"

Nikki sighed. "We went to the restaurant where she

97

works, and remember how I was concerned that she wouldn't want anything to do with us? It seems I was justified."

"Oh no," Ava lamented. "What did she say?"

"She said she doesn't want anything to do with us and asked why, after all this time, am I coming to tell her she's adopted when her real mother is on the verge of death."

"Wow," Ava exclaimed. "I'm sorry, hon, but I'm sure she was just angry. She couldn't mean any of that."

"She sounded sincere to me," Nikki replied. "Although, in hindsight, she was having a rough night, and some guy was harassing her over the menu."

"There you go," Ava replied. "She was having a bad night, and you just probably picked the worst time to drop a bomb like that. Maybe you should just give her some time."

"That's what Paul said." Nikki sighed again.

"Paul's a smart man," Ava said.

"Should I call her? Check on her?"

"Babe, this is not something you can force on someone. Just imagine how you would feel if someone just walked up to you and told you that you're adopted. Would you just leap for joy?"

"I guess not," Nikki replied. "I hope she comes around is all."

"She will," Ava told her. "But how are things on the other end? How's Trish and the Nestled Inn?"

"Trish is the same," Nikki replied as she sipped from her cup. "Every day, the doctors hope, and we hope, but all we can do is pray and wait. Reed, one of the guys from the Humane Society, wants to host an event for her this coming weekend to get support and offer prayers for her recovery."

"Well, that's nice," Ava said happily. "I wish I could come, but I'll be tied up."

"It's okay," Nikki told her. "I know you'd be here if you could."

"And how about Paul?" Ava teased. "Anything going on there?"

"Nothing since the last time you checked." Nikki laughed.

"Bummer. I'm still rooting for you. He seems like a good guy."

"He is, but now's not the time. I don't think any time will be the time for that, so I'm not getting my hopes up again only to be let down hard."

"I hear you," Ava replied. "At least you have your job to distract you."

"Speaking of which, I have an investigative piece to finish, but I have another day or so. Luckily, I don't need to be at the office to do my job."

"Yeah, you're lucky. I still have to go to work and have so many chores this weekend."

Nikki laughed. "What's new?"

"Yeah, what's new? And with that said, I have to run," Ava said. "Lots to do. I just wanted to check in on you and make sure everything is okay."

"Thanks, hon." Nikki smiled. "I'll talk to you later."

After Ava hung up, Nikki lazed around the house. She couldn't even call Amy if she wanted to because she didn't have a phone number for her. Plus, she would probably drive her away, as Paul had said.

But she couldn't remain content for the rest of the day. The following day began in no better way than the one before, but she had to busy herself so the time would pass quickly.

Kaylyn was heading to the laundry area when Nikki ran into her on her way through the back door.

"Hello, ma'am." Kaylyn smiled and embraced Nikki.

"Didn't I tell you to call me Nikki?" she replied as she pulled back. "No more of this ma'am thing."

Kaylyn laughed. "Were you coming to find me?"

"Yes, actually," Nikki replied. "I wanted to check in on things."

"You can walk with me." Kaylyn started moving again.

"How are the reservations stacking up?" Nikki asked. "Where are we going?"

"Heading to the laundry." Kaylyn glanced back and replied, "I just wanted to track our inventory. We have every room booked as it is and five others waiting to get a room."

"Wow. Quite the buzz, eh?" Nikki said with pride.

"It really gets busy here in the summertime. A little slower in the winter, but we've always had a full house." They got to the laundry room, and Kaylyn showed Nikki where the cleaning supplies and towels were kept. "Dorothy does the laundry on Mondays, but it seems we need to get fresh towels, miniature shampoo and body washes for the baths, toiletries, and there was one room that needed deep cleaning—there was a wine spill, so we need supplies for that as well. But all in all, things are going well. Don't you worry about it ma...Nikki." She grinned when she remembered Nikki's earlier warning.

"That's good news," Nikki said, breathing a sigh of relief. "I'm glad Trish has such reliable and capable people around. That's a blessing."

"Indeed," Kaylyn agreed as they walked out of the room and back into the hallway.

"And speaking of blessings, I have a little bittersweet news to share," Nikki said, and her shoulders sagged.

Kaylyn noticed and stopped her by holding her arm. "What news? Is it Trish?"

"No, it's not her, but it concerns her daughter. We found her, and Paul and I went to visit her on Friday evening."

Kaylyn's eyes lit up, and she clapped her hands. "That's good news indeed," she said happily. "Trish is going to be delighted." Then she noticed Nikki's downcast eyes. "It didn't go well with her?"

Nikki shook her head, and tears welled in her eyes again. "No, not so well."

"What happened?"

"She didn't take the news well," Nikki said without relaying the entire awful scene.

"Oh," Kaylyn replied. "Well, just give her some time. She might come around."

Nikki laughed. "That seems to be the general consensus. I guess that's all I can do."

"The good thing is you found her, and now she knows. Based on my experience, people don't just walk away from something like that."

"I hope you're right," Nikki told her.

"Come, let's get you something to eat. You're beginning to look a little pale," Kaylyn said in a matronly way.

Nikki was grateful because she hadn't eaten all day. When she returned to the house, she got to work on the paper she needed to submit, and as she did, she started to bake. Cooking had always been another passion of hers, so she tried to busy her mind with writing and getting a savory meat pie in the oven.

The house was filled with the flavors coming from her

seasoning and spices, and once out of the oven, she set her pie on the counter, just inside the sliding window, to cool. Her stomach had started to rumble, and she anticipated digging into her creation.

She was finishing her paper when she heard a scratching by the window. She knitted her brows as she walked cautiously to the kitchen to investigate. She peered outside and noticed a cat reaching toward the window, paws scratching as it tried to get a piece of the pie.

Nikki smiled. "Oh, you like the smell too, don't you?" she asked the animal as she slid the window open. "I guess we could share."

She reached for the animal and was surprised when it calmly came toward her. She enticed it with the pie and brought it to the back door where it could feed. She watched it as it ate hungrily and noticed it was a little thin, with its fur pasted on, like it had gotten caught in something sticky. There were no name tags, and she suspected it was a stray cat.

After it was done eating, she took on the task of cleaning it up. That was a bit of a struggle, and she realized all too quickly that cats really didn't like water much. She managed to get it decent-looking.

The thought occurred to her that she could take it to the Humane Society. She was glad for yet another distraction as she drove to the shelter.

"Nikki," Reed greeted her upon arrival. "What do we have here?"

"Oh, just a little friend that wandered onto my windowsill today. You think you can make a home for her here?"

Reed's jaw dropped. "Sorry, Nikki. We're out of space at the moment."

"Oh, okay. But I can't just let it go now," she said as she looked at the very calm animal. She couldn't imagine how it was a stray.

Reed grinned at her. "Maybe you can keep it."

"Keep it?" Nikki asked in surprise.

"Just until we have more space. People adopt animals all the time. I'm sure we'll have a space in no time."

Nikki sighed and looked at the cat as it yawned and prepared to take a snooze. "It is kinda cute. Okay, I'll keep it. For now."

"I'm glad you came over," Reed said. "I meant to call you but got caught up."

"What's up?" Nikki asked and started to stroke the cat in her arms.

"I just wanted to keep you in the loop about this weekend," he beamed. "Everything is in place. We've sent word to practically everyone with ears or eyes."

Nikki laughed. "We'll have the place all set. I can't wait. Thanks again, Reed."

"Anytime," he said.

And Nikki returned home with her new friend. He sat on the front seat with his head on his paws, and she reached over and occasionally stroked it as she drove.

It would seem she had planned on staying in Camano for a short time, but as the days passed, she felt like she was slowly setting her roots.

She was in much better spirits when she pulled into the driveway but then slammed on the brakes when she saw Amy sitting on the front steps with a suitcase next to her.

Chapter Thirteen

Nikki couldn't get out of the car fast enough, and she was halfway to Amy when she remembered the cat.

She hurried back for the animal before she returned to her niece once more. She expected a phone call—not a trip, and certainly not a suitcase.

"Amy? What's wrong?"

"You said I could come," she said in a shaky voice.

"Yeah, sure. I meant that. Come on in," Nikki said as she looked around, half expecting to see the reason Amy was there with a suitcase.

She got up, and Nikki picked up the suitcase and followed her to the front door.

"Here, have a seat," Nikki said and pointed at the living room once they were inside.

"I'm going to give Tabby some milk or something. I just found her this morning. I think Tabby is a pretty name for her."

"It seems you're pretty good at finding lost things," Amy muttered.

Nikki had been in investigative journalism for too long to miss all the signals Amy threw her way. She was in trouble—there was no reason for her to have run off if she wasn't, and it concerned Nikki. Her suitcase presently nestled at her feet was enough of an indication that she was running from something. Instantly, Nikki's mind returned to the man at the restaurant, and she hurried back to her niece as quickly as she could.

"I didn't want to believe you," Amy said softly when Nikki returned and sat on the sofa across from her.

Nikki didn't interrupt her. She watched her as she toyed with her fingers and stared at the floor—almost the same way Trish had appeared before she had given her up so many years ago. The scene was almost unreal for Nikki, so she waited and allowed Amy to take the lead on what happened next.

"What you told me didn't make sense," she eventually said and raised her head, although she avoided Nikki's gaze. "About being adopted, but somehow it made sense." She stared at the wall and spoke like she was reciting the scene of a play. "So many times, I thought that there was no way I came from *them,*" she said as her lips contorted, like just the thought of her parents left a bitter aftertaste. "Still, I didn't think I was adopted." It was then that she looked Nikki in the eyes. "Why didn't she want me?"

Nikki's heart broke as she saw Amy's glassy eyes. "It wasn't that," she replied softly. "She wanted you very much. *I* wanted you!"

"So why did she give me away? To live with monsters?" Amy asked and quickly brushed away a tear.

Nikki's maternal instincts kicked into gear, and she walked over to sit next to Amy. "Honey, you have no idea how much she wanted you, but she didn't have a choice."

Amy got up and walked toward the window. "Everyone has a choice. How can you give away your kid?"

Nikki knew she had to go back to the beginning for Amy to understand. "Back then, Trish had gotten pregnant by a boy who wanted nothing to do with her afterward, and my parents..." Nikki said as she recalled the bitter yet vivid memories. "They didn't want their reputation damaged by a young daughter who had gotten pregnant and would be a single mother. She was only nineteen, and our father forced her to leave Seattle for Arlington, have the baby, give it up for adoption, and then return like nothing had happened. It was right before I found out I wouldn't be able to have children," she said and watched as Amy studied her face for the truth. "I begged them to let me have you instead because I was already married. They refused. They wouldn't let us keep you, but make no mistake—you were wanted. By us both."

"You could have done more. You knew where I was being kept. Why couldn't you have just come for me there?" Amy asked.

"You have no idea how many times over the years I've beat myself up with that same question. My parents didn't have to know. No one had to. But it didn't feel right going behind Trish's back with something like that, so I did nothing. And it wasn't easy, Amy. You have to believe me."

"You all just gave me up and then lived happily ever after. Meanwhile, I was stuck with a drunk who kept hitting my mother," Amy said as her brows dipped in anger.

"Far from it," Nikki said and smoothed her hair back. She stared at the ceiling, her hands tucked under her legs while she continued to sit, as she recalled the moment that shattered the family. "We were never the same after that. I went back to Arlington, and I never returned, not until I heard that our parents had died in an accident in Mexico. That was ten years ago and was the first time I'd even seen Trish since that day."

Amy grew quiet as she listened to Nikki.

"I never forgave Trish for not letting me have you, and I was so bitter toward her. For years," Nikki said in disbelief. "We lived an hour away from each other, and I didn't reach out to her. Not once." She sank onto the chair as grief enveloped her. "The next thing I knew, she was in an accident, and the doctors had to induce a coma to keep her alive. I may never see my sister again, but she wanted this. Finding you. For us to reconnect."

"I'm kind of tired," Amy said abruptly. "Can I...is it okay to stay here? I don't think I want to face my parents again."

"Sure," Nikki said as she flew up. "There's a spare room upstairs at the end of the hall. Make yourself at home and stay for as long as you'd like. I'll check on you in a minute."

"Okay. Thanks," Amy replied gingerly. She walked off and glanced back at Nikki when she reached the stairs. Nikki could tell her story hadn't landed on deaf ears—there was a hint of pity in Amy's eyes.

Retelling the story had only served to awaken the fear and hurt inside Nikki, and after Amy was upstairs, she walked to the kitchen as fresh tears ran down her face. Tabby rubbed against her leg, and she was glad she had that source of comfort.

When she looked in on Amy before bed, she was curled up in a fetal position, and it melted her heart. She

107

only wished Trish would wake up so she could experience her own daughter.

The following morning, Nikki was in high spirits. She hadn't bothered to make breakfast since she'd been there, but Amy inspired her. She was up early, dancing to Pharrell's "Happy" as she made a garden omelet, breakfast muffins, sausage, and toast.

"Good morning," a still sleepy Amy said as she walked into the kitchen.

"Oh, morning. Come, have a seat," Nikki said as she opened the cupboard and took down some plates.

"Smells great," Amy commented as Nikki lifted an omelet onto a plate for her.

"Thank you," Nikki replied as she joined her by the counter.

Amy took a small bite before it turned to much bigger ones. "These are really good," she exclaimed. "You're a really good cook."

"Yeah, it's one of my passions." Nikki shrugged.

"Mine too." Amy smiled. "I've always wanted to be a pastry chef."

"I guess it runs in the family, then," Nikki dared to add, and Amy smiled wider as she dug into her meal. "Speaking of family, I need to take you to see Trish's lawyer."

"Lawyer? Why? I thought you said she's in a coma," Amy replied and scrunched up her face.

"She is, but she made provisions just in case..." Nikki trailed off. "There are things you need to know."

"Such as?" Amy questioned.

"You'll know soon enough," Nikki told her. "We'll go to see him as soon as we're done eating. But first, I want to take you on a tour of the Nestled Inn."

"Why?" Amy asked again, like a child.

"I thought you were past the age of 'whys.'" Nikki laughed. "It's your mother's place. I thought you'd want to see it."

Amy shrugged. "I guess. I'm already here."

Kaylyn, Dorothy, and the rest of the staff were elated to see her.

"Oh, this makes me so happy," Kaylyn gushed as she pulled a frightened Amy into a bear hug.

Everyone gathered around her and commented on Trish and how happy she will be to meet Amy. Nikki could see how uncomfortable Amy was becoming, so she excused them and instead took her on a small tour.

"This is a one Michelin star restaurant?" Amy asked in surprise when she walked into the restaurant.

"It is," Nikki told her as they stood just inside the pristine establishment. "Lot 28. It has a mother restaurant across town. Paul, our childhood friend, was kind enough to give Trish his name to get her on solid ground. Business has been great since." Then Nikki turned to face Amy. "You know, you could learn a thing or two here."

"Maybe," Amy said.

"Oh, look at the time," Nikki exclaimed. "We need to get going. Come on."

Amy wasn't as enthusiastic about going with Nikki, and Nikki was apprehensive about the trip. She wasn't sure how Amy would react to Trish's wishes, but she could only hope for the best.

"Good morning." Frank smiled as he opened his office door. "Come in. Have a seat."

Amy walked in tentatively, followed by Nikki. They'd barely sat down when Frank pulled out the file. "I know you don't want to be here longer than you should," he said and looked at Amy. "You're a very lucky young woman." He smiled. "I'm happy to meet you."

Amy smiled weakly and glanced across at Nikki. "Thanks. What's this about? I thought these things were meant for, you know, the deceased."

"Sometimes," Frank confirmed. "Other times, you can appoint a personal representative or give someone power of attorney while you're still alive. In this case, your mother, Trish," he said and glanced at her over his glasses, "has treated this like a will."

"Okay," Amy replied tentatively and settled into her chair.

"Okay," Nikki breathed. "Let's hear it."

It was a nervous occasion for them both, and although Nikki knew what Frank was about to say, she was still anxious about how Amy would react.

Frank read Trish's request concerning Amy's and Nikki's acquisition of the Nestled Inn and the clause that Amy had to run the establishment for a year alongside Nikki.

"Wait, what?" Amy asked and turned to Nikki. "You knew about this, didn't you?"

"Yes," Nikki replied.

Amy scoffed. "Unbelievable. And here I was thinking that you had come to find me so we could 'reconnect,'" she mocked, using air quotes. "You just wanted a pansy— someone to carry on the business because *Mom* can't," she said with disdain and crossed her arms. "No!" she said emphatically.

"Amy, it's not like that," Nikki tried to explain. "She didn't want to lock you in for life, so she just wanted to give you a year to test things out. And that's not the only reason she wanted to find you."

"It's just a coincidence that I wasn't found until now, though, right? You know what?" she said and got up. "I don't want anything to do with this. The two of you can go and find another daughter she might have given up."

And with that, she stormed out of the office, leaving a perplexed Frank staring at an even more confused Nikki.

Chapter Fourteen

Paul was getting ready to head out in his boat for an early morning ride when his phone rang.

It had to be the restaurant. That was his first thought. *Or Sarah!*

He made a mad dash for the device and breathed a sigh of relief when he saw it wasn't Sarah.

"Hello?" he answered cautiously.

"Paul, sorry to wake you," Ken, his head chef, said on the other end.

He knew it. It had to be the restaurant.

"You didn't. What's wrong?"

Ken chuckled lightly. "You were always so insightful."

"It's not every day I get a call from my head chef at six in the morning," Paul replied.

Right away, a bout of coughing gripped Ken, and Paul knew why he had called. "You're sick?"

"Yeah," Ken replied. "I got bit by the flu bug. I'm afraid I'll have to be out for a couple of days."

"That's alright, man," Paul replied with understanding. "There's nothing you can do about it."

"Do you think you can maybe take over for me? For just a few days?"

"It's too late to get anyone else anyway," Paul replied. "Don't worry about it. I'll figure something out. Feel better."

"Thanks, man," Ken said and hung up in the middle of a cough.

Paul stood by the doorway as excitement and trepidations swirled inside him. It was far too late to get another qualified chef. He would have to take over at the restaurant. It wasn't something he'd done full-time since he'd discovered he had a heart condition.

But it had to be done.

His hands shook as he put on his chef whites and prepared to go to the restaurant later that morning. He chose not to announce to his staff before he arrived, so they were surprised and elated when they saw him walking into the kitchen dressed for work.

"Aw, man." Will laughed. "Don't tell me you're coming back," he joked.

Paul chuckled. "Just for a couple of days. Ken has the flu."

"Oh," Will replied with a shocked expression. "I hope it isn't bad."

"It sounded like it," Paul replied sorrowfully. "But he's tough. He'll be back here bossing you around in no time. For now, I'll be that guy." He grinned.

"Good to have you back," Will replied. "I'll try to take it easy on you."

Paul laughed. "I'll be fine. Now, what do we have in the refrigerator?" he asked as he moved away and toward the walk-in refrigerator. He felt a rush of excitement as his staff followed him, and they checked the menu and pantry items.

A deep yearning overwhelmed him as he walked back into the kitchen. He loved cooking and hated that he couldn't do it all the time, on account of his heart. But his health came first, and he had to abide by the advice of his doctor and his daughter.

His heart was racing when the customers started walking in, and the first of the orders began to pour in.

Paul took the order from Lexi, who gave him a broad smile. "Welcome back, boss," she said.

"It's not like I wasn't here," Paul reminded her.

"You know what I mean." She winked.

He smiled and turned to the chefs. "Table four, two scallops and one tamarind glazed chicken wings. Table two, one lobster bisque and clam chowder."

"Heard, Chef," Will replied and got to work.

"What's the time on the scallops and wings?" Paul asked.

"Eight minutes, Chef," Will replied as he reached for the ingredients.

Paul started on the clam chowder and felt like his old self again, even as more orders came in. He relished giving the orders and checking the plates for perfection. He tasted every dish that was prepared and only sent out the ones he thought were Michelin-starred quality.

They worked feverishly throughout lunch and into dinner, and at no point did he feel overwhelmed. He was in his element, and he loved it.

Every so often, he ventured into the dining room to meet some of his guests when things slowed down for a few minutes.

"I knew something was different about the dinner

today," Simon, one of his resident customers, declared when he walked over to them. "I didn't know you were back. I hope you're staying."

"Are you suggesting my chefs don't know what they're doing?"

Simon laughed. "Not at all. But Chef Gordon Ramsay's chef isn't Chef Gordon Ramsay if you catch my drift."

Paul laughed. "Well, thank you for the compliment. I'm glad you're enjoying the experience."

"As always," he replied. "The chowder was superb. Not to mention the beef Wellington. Melts in the mouth."

Paul's heart was full as he walked around the restaurant, giving most of the customers a personalized experience. It was just getting dark outside, and the low-hanging lamps gave off a romantic appeal. The rustic brick finish added a nice country feel to the place, and he observed the floral white centerpieces amid glistening silver accessories on each table.

Lot 28 was written on the far walls in cursive black and red lettering, and he felt pride in his accomplishment as he returned to the kitchen.

They were in full swing for dinner, sending out one order after another. Several times, he had to enter the dining room to greet another customer who heard he was on duty, but that was no surprise to Paul.

It was on one of those visits to the dining room that he ran into his daughter.

"Dad, what are you doing here?" she hissed as she leaned closer to him.

"How did you know I was here?" he asked. "Debbi," he replied as he looked around for the server. She could at least have given him a heads-up.

"Yes, Debbi," Sarah snapped.

Paul looked across at Aaron. "It's good to see you."

Aaron nodded and smiled at him. "Should you be here at all?"

"I heard he's been here all day," Sarah said angrily. "Dad, what are you thinking? You know what the doctor said."

"Honey, now is not the time for this," Paul said as he looked around and hoped no one had overheard their conversation.

It was no news to the frequent customers that he had to take a medical leave a few years back, but he had always been around for a few hours most days even though he had mainly been supervising things.

"There shouldn't be a conversation about this," Sarah snapped.

"Boss," Lexi said as she came up to him. "You're needed in the kitchen."

"Thanks, Lexi," Paul said and looked at Sarah. "I know you're worried, but I'm not back here full time. It's just for a few days."

"Dad, you can't handle the daily stress, even for one day," Sarah whined.

"I can't say I disagree," Aaron chimed in. "It was pretty bad that time."

"Ugh!" Sarah groaned. "I can't," she said, slapping her napkin onto the table. "I need some air."

"Sarah," Paul called after her.

Aaron sprang from his chair. "I'll calm her down. Go do what you have to."

Paul's spirit sank as he walked back to the kitchen. He was not his usual happy-go-lucky self after the confrontation with Sarah. He had hoped she wouldn't have found out about it.

"Sorry, boss," Debbi said as she walked up to him. "I didn't know she didn't know you're back. It slipped."

"It's okay, Debbi," Paul told her. "Let's get back to work. We're filling up over here."

Ironically, even though Sarah was mad at him for being back at work, and he hated that he had disappointed her, cooking relaxed him the most. In seconds, as he pounded steak and ground lamb into sausages, he'd forgotten his earlier fight.

Debbi informed him that Sarah had returned to her table, and he had no doubt she was still fuming. When things settled down, he returned to her.

"Come here," he told her, and the three walked to the back patio.

He could see that she had been crying. Her mascara had smudged under her eyes, and she pulled away when he tried to hug her.

"No," she whimpered. "Dad, I remember it like it was yesterday," she said and tapped her chest. "You could have died, and now you're back here like it doesn't even matter."

"Sweetheart, it wasn't planned," he explained. "Ken got the flu, and it was too late to find anyone, so I had to come in. How professional would it be if I didn't?"

"I don't care," Sarah cried. "You're the only parent I have. What if you experienced another heart attack?"

"But I didn't," Paul said in his defense. "I know the warning signs now, and you have no idea how good it feels to be back. Even for a couple of days."

"Dad, you didn't see it coming the last time," Sarah cried.

"The heart attack wasn't life-threatening, honey. Aaron, help me out here," Paul pleaded with the man.

Aaron shrugged. "I agree with her. The first time isn't usually the one to worry about. It can get worse."

Paul groaned.

"He's right," Sarah chimed in. "The next time, you could die! Is that what you want? To die and make me an orphan?" she asked as tears rolled down her cheeks, and she brushed them away. "I already lost Mom. I can't lose you, too."

Paul's chest tightened as he watched his baby girl crying over him. He would do anything to protect her, but he felt like his hands were bound. He reached for her, and that time, she allowed him to pull her into a firm embrace.

She sobbed against his chest, dampening his chef whites with her tears. Her body rocked in his arms and broke his heart.

"It's alright," he whispered against her head. "I'm still here, and I'm not going anywhere, so you can quit worrying, okay. It's just for a few days. The last time, I was here all the time and stressed over a lot of things. It's not the same this time around. I know better now, and like I said, it's only until Ken gets better."

"Are you sure?" she asked as she pulled away. "I don't want you to sit at home and be miserable all the time. That's not what I'm saying, but I was surprised when I came in and realized you were here."

"I know you mean well, and I'm sorry I didn't tell you, but it happened so fast."

"Would you have told me anyway?" She stared into his face.

He grinned at her. "Probably not, but that's only because I know you would worry about me. I don't want

118

you to worry. I want you to go out and have fun and think about the wedding."

"I know you have a lot more to do at the Nestled Inn now that Trish is in the hospital. I just don't want you overdoing it."

"Nikki's doing a great job at the inn, so it's not as hard as you think, and I promise not to overdo it. Now, can I go back inside and do what I love?"

Sarah smiled at him. "Fine. But I'll be watching you."

"I consider myself warned," Paul said as he kissed her forehead, patted Aaron on the shoulder, and walked back inside the Lot 28 restaurant.

He was beginning to feel like his old self again.

Chapter Fifteen

Paul was in better spirits for the rest of the evening as he whistled tunes while preparing meals and calling out orders.

He hadn't felt so alive in what felt like forever. He had just walked through his door when his phone rang. His face lit up even more when he saw that it was Nikki.

"Hello," he answered in a singsong voice.

"Someone sounds like they're in a good mood," Nikki said on the other end.

"That's because I sort of am," Paul said and kicked off his loafers. "I went back to the restaurant today, and I'll be there for a couple of days."

"How come?"

"Ken's sick," he told her and headed for the kitchen. "It's just for a few days, but I can't tell you how good it feels."

Nikki laughed. "I can just imagine."

"Why did you call? What's going on? Any trouble at the inn?"

"Oh no, nothing like that. Everything's great. It's Amy."

Paul sat on the sofa with the bottle of water in his free hand. "Amy? What about her?"

"She's here," Nikki told him. "She came back after we visited her in Seattle."

"Really? That's great news," he exclaimed.

"Not really," Nikki groaned. "I took her to see Frank, and she freaked out."

"Freaked out? Why?"

"I don't know. She thinks that the only reason we came to find her was so we could use her to take over the Nestled Inn and restaurant," Nikki explained.

"But that's not true," Paul replied. "Trish started to look for her long before the accident."

"I know that," Nikki said. "Try telling that to her. She thinks I just want to fulfill my sister's dying wish."

Paul sighed. "Okay, what if I come over tomorrow and talk to her? She might listen to me."

"It's worth a shot," Nikki replied. "I'd appreciate that. She's already getting her things together. She might leave in the morning."

"I'll be over early in the morning, then," Paul told her.

He could imagine how frustrated Nikki might feel. She had been thrust into a life that she didn't understand and one that demanded so much from her. She was doing the best she could, but the whole plan to find Amy had started with him and Trish. He couldn't let Amy just walk away without trying.

The following morning, he was there at the crack of dawn. He was relieved when Amy opened the door.

"Hi, good morning," he said.

She rolled her eyes rudely. "If you're here to see

Nikki, she's not here. She went to the inn or whatever," she said and walked back inside the house.

"I'm not here to see Nikki," Paul said and walked in after her. "I'm here to see you." He looked around and saw her suitcase leaning against the wall. "Going somewhere?"

"You were with Nikki in Seattle, right?" she asked.

"Yeah," he said and folded his arms, careful not to come too close to her for fear of intimidating her and spooking her even further. "Your mother—Trish—is a very dear friend of mine, and I know you're a little confused, but just hear me out for a second."

"Why? What are you going to say that's different from what Nikki said?" She crossed her arms.

"That's what I'm going to tell you," he said and motioned to the front porch. "I'm not going to force you to stay. You can still leave if you want to, but just hear what I have to say."

Amy sighed. "Fine." Her shoulders sagged as she walked out onto the front porch. "Okay. What do you want to tell me?"

Paul joined her on the opposite end of the porch swing. "I've known your mother for a long time, and it wasn't just a few times that she's mentioned you."

"Ugh," Amy groaned. "Don't tell me how much she loved and missed me but didn't even try to find me."

"But she did," Paul pointed out. "She spoke about you many times and how much she hurt that she was forced to give you up. She hasn't had any other children since, so you were it."

"That was her choice," Amy replied coldly.

"I know you're upset, but you can't blame her. She was young and confused, and she didn't want to find you and disrupt your life, so she waited. About a year ago, it got unbearable for her, so she hired a private investigator to find you. She didn't have the accident until after, so it wasn't like she had any kind of ulterior motive in finding you."

"Well, how did she make the will, then?"

Paul sighed. "That was just something she wanted to do. She and Nikki had drifted apart for years, and she wanted a way to bring the two of you closer, so she thought this might be it. It was only days before the accident that she asked Frank to adjust her will just in case anything happened to her. It was like she knew," Paul said with a sigh.

Amy grew extremely quiet as they stared at the rolling waves crashing against the shore. "I'm sorry that she was in an accident."

"Me too," Paul replied, glancing at Amy as he offered her a quick but sorrowful smile. "I miss her. She was really something."

"If she and Nikki weren't close, why did she ask her to come and find me if anything happened to her?"

"Because despite everything that happened between them, she knew how much Nikki loved and wanted you. Their bond was broken over you, Amy. She knew Nikki would never deny her something so special. Or herself."

Amy hung her head as she stared at the floorboards. "Maybe Nikki is just acting out of guilt, then."

"She isn't," Paul told her. "She wouldn't have placed her life on hold to do this out of guilt. I would know—I've known her a long time. And she's torn up about the fact that you want to leave. She really wants you here with her."

"I don't know what to believe anymore," Amy said

sadly as her eyes got glossy. "My life has not been ideal, and I've struggled a lot. I just wish..." She swallowed hard.

Paul didn't need her to finish the sentence to understand what she was saying. "I know," he told her. "Believe me. I have a daughter who is barely older than you, and she lost her mother when she was only twelve years old. That was a pretty tough time for her and for me, and I made a lot of mistakes. But my point is, we all have something to deal with in one way or another. We can only do the best with what we have now, and what's best for you is to give Nikki a chance. You won't regret it."

Amy looked over at Paul and raised her brows at him. "Okay, which one of them were you in love with?"

Paul laughed at her question, mainly because it took him by surprise. "To be honest, Nikki and I dated back in high school, but there's nothing between her or Trish and me right now. I'm just trying to help out some friends of mine."

"Doing your civic duty, huh?" Amy smiled.

"You could say that," he said. "Did it work? Will you stay?"

"Uh, I guess so," she replied. "But I'm not making any promises. I just want to stay to get some questions answered and figure out who I am."

"Fair enough," Paul told her. "And just so you know, you're welcome at my restaurant anytime. I'd love for you to meet my daughter. I think the two of you would make good friends."

"Yeah?" Amy asked hopefully.

"I think so," Paul replied. "Is it okay to leave now and not worry that you'll hightail it out of here?"

Amy laughed, and the mellow sound of her voice reminded him of her mother. "I'll be around."

"Good," he said and got up. "I have to head over to my restaurant. Is it okay to check in on you sometimes?"

"Sure," she replied.

He'd just got up out of the swing when Nikki pulled into the driveway. "Oh, here comes Nikki. She'll be glad you're staying. Later, kiddo," he said as he walked down the steps and over to Nikki.

"What happened?" she asked anxiously as she got out of the car and slammed the door shut.

"Um, I think she's going to stay," Paul told her happily. He thought she'd receive the news well but detected something darker in her tone.

"What did you say to her?" she asked with a hint of accusation.

"I told her how much her mother loves her and has always wanted her, and that you do too. You're not here to use her but to make sure she'll be alright. Along those lines," he said to her. "What's wrong?"

"Why did she listen to you and not to me?" Nikki asked. "I said those very same things to her last night, and she packed her bags anyway."

"I'm not sure," Paul replied with apprehension.

"What exactly did you say to her?" Nikki accused.

"Nikki, I know you might be frustrated, but please don't do this. Just be happy she's decided to stay. Don't make something out of this when you don't have to."

"I'm not trying to make anything out of this," she snapped, then glanced at the patio to check if Amy was observing her interaction. "You're making me look bad in front of her."

Paul threw his hands in the air. "I'm not doing this

right now," he said, stepping back. "I have to go to the restaurant. Let me know if you need anything."

She hadn't replied by the time Paul walked away. He wasn't sure what she was going on about, but he sensed an air of jealousy about her. There was no need for it because he wasn't trying to get between them, and she had been fine with him coming over to talk some sense into Amy just the night before.

He wasn't sure what changed in her. Maybe everything was finally taking a toll on her. He refused to blame Nikki for it. He'd give her some time and space to calm down. Maybe when she connected with Amy, she'd be in better spirits.

But from all indications, it was better for him to maintain his distance at present.

Chapter Sixteen

J ust as soon as Paul drove off, guilt washed over Nikki.

She had been a little jealous that Paul had gotten through to Amy when she couldn't even though Amy was her niece. Her pride wouldn't allow her to call him and apologize. Besides, she still had to deal with Amy.

"You're staying after all," she said as she met her just inside the front door.

"Yeah," she replied casually.

"What made you change your mind?" Nikki asked curiously as the green snake of envy retreated very slowly.

Amy shrugged. "Curiosity? I wanted to know more about my real family, and Paul was pretty convincing."

"Oh," Nikki said, then walked to the kitchen. "Have you eaten yet?"

"Look, I don't want to be a burden," Amy said, following her into the kitchen. "I'm used to making my own way. I've been working since I was sixteen. I can help out."

Nikki waved her off and opened the fridge door. "That won't be necessary. We have everything taken care of."

"No," Amy insisted. "I want to help. I can get a job to help with the bills or food or something."

Nikki's heart was lifted when she heard her speak like that. She had plans to stay for a while to be responsible, but she was curious about why Amy left Seattle in the first place. But she tabled that thought for a different time.

"As far as I know, the Nestled Inn and the restaurant take care of the mortgage for the properties and the utilities. If you want to get something for yourself, then that's fine, but this place is as much yours as it's mine now. You don't need to earn it."

"I'm not trying to earn it. I just want to be useful," Amy replied. "I've seen what leeching off others can do." She got a faraway look in her eyes like she recalled a painful memory.

Nikki sighed and placed the carton of juice on the counter. "Fine," she said and finally gave in. She could understand Amy's need for independence. It didn't have anything to do with the money. The same spirit ran in both Nikki's and Trish's veins. "How about we go see what they can do at the restaurant?"

"Great!" Amy said and rubbed her hands together. "You already know I can wait tables, and I'd really love to shadow any pastry chef who's around—you know, to hone my skills."

Nikki smiled. "I'll see what I can do. I don't think there's a pastry chef at Lot 28, though, but I'll have to check again."

"Maybe Paul knows someone," Amy replied with

great excitement, and Nikki watched as her eyes lit up like a kid in a candy store.

"Maybe," Nikki said. "We can ask him, but I can't make any promises. I'm not sure what's possible yet."

"That's okay. There are other places in town, right?"

"True," Nikki agreed. "Let's go see the head chef later and hear what he has to say. I wish you didn't feel the need to work, though."

"What else am I going to do while I'm here?" Amy asked and sipped from the glass Nikki passed to her. "I can't just sit here every day or surf to pass the time."

Nikki laughed. "You make a good point."

She loved how easy it was getting for them to have a conversation. She knew that things would be seamless in time, and it would be as if she'd never been away from them. She just wished that Trish would wake up to see it.

Later that morning, the two women ventured over to the Nestled Inn.

"I have to say, this is a really nice spot," Amy complimented as they walked through the lobby. "Trish has great taste." She admired the oversized vases sitting in the corners with green ferns sticking out of them, which greatly contrasted the pastel-colored walls. The reception desk had tulips and daffodils adorning it, and the burnt-orange, beige, and brown color block carpeting was the perfect finish.

"Hello, you two," Kaylyn greeted them as they walked by.

"Hi, Kaylyn," Nikki replied.

Amy smiled and waved, but she didn't utter a word.

Amy was even more in awe when she walked into the restaurant. It had the same rustic appeal as the mother restaurant, bearing the intimate low-hanging lights above the dining tables, potted plants sat in blocks next to columns that had the same brick overlay, and the tables were pristine with silver accessories atop off-white linen.

"I would love to work here," Amy gushed. "The tips must be awesome."

Nikki laughed. "I bet."

The restaurant wasn't open yet, but the head chef, William, was already there prepping things.

He wiped his hands on the towel draped over his shoulder before he extended it to Nikki. "Nice to see you. And who's this?" he asked as he took Amy's hand.

"This is Amy, Trish's daughter," Nikki said and cleared her throat, mainly because she didn't know if Amy wanted to be announced as Trish's daughter just yet.

"Oh," he beamed, and the dimple in his chin deepened with the twinkle in his gray eyes. "Well then, it's a great pleasure."

"Thanks." Amy blushed and looked across at Nikki.

"What brings the two of you over? Not that I'm complaining, but you're usually here a little later in the day," William said, adjusting his head's hat. Traces of his raven-black hair showed around the sides and back, and his clean-shaven face gave him a boyish look despite being almost forty years old.

"Well, we were wondering if you know of any job vacancies here," Nikki began. "Amy's trying to get a job."

"Oh," he said and then stroked his chin. "I don't think we have any openings now. If we were to give you a job here, we'd have to let someone go."

"No, no, that's not necessary," Amy replied right away. "I don't want to take anyone's job. I can look elsewhere."

"Are you sure?" William asked.

"Yes," Amy replied.

"Well, thanks anyway, Will," Nikki said.

"Maybe you can ask Paul," William suggested. "His restaurant is busier."

"That's what I was thinking," Nikki replied even though she wasn't looking forward to seeing Paul again that day. She had been rude earlier, and the feeling wasn't sitting pretty with her. "Thanks again."

"Anytime," William said, returning to his duties.

"Is the other restaurant like this one?" Amy asked once they were in the car.

"Pretty much," Nikki replied. "This one is miniature-sized compared to Paul's. They have the same decor and settings."

"Nice." Amy smiled as she stared out the window.

Nikki wasn't sure what was going on in Amy's mind or when she might decide to leave, so she wanted to take the opportunity to introduce her to Trish.

"Hey, so I was thinking," she began tentatively as her heart thumped. "I was planning to visit Trish again later today. How about you come with me so you can meet her."

Amy didn't respond for a couple of seconds. "Didn't you say she's in a coma?"

"Yeah, but the doctors said that she might still be able to hear what's going on around her. I know she'd be happy to hear your voice if that's true."

"That would be kind of weird for me," Amy replied softly. "Maybe another time."

The disappointment hit Nikki hard, but she couldn't disclose how much. She understood what Amy said, but she had really hoped she would agree to that.

"Is that going to be a problem?" Amy turned to her and asked matter-of-factly. "Like, is that a condition to my staying at the house?"

"No," Nikki replied emphatically. "I know that's not something either of us can rush, so I'll let you go at your own pace, but I'm not going to force you to go or chase you out if you don't. Like I said, the house and inn are yours too. Legally, no one can chase you out of either of them."

She was almost sure she saw a sigh of relief escape Amy before she turned her face once more to the window and avoided Nikki's eyes.

That was just as well. Nikki didn't want her to see the first signs of tears that she had to quickly blink away.

Paul greeted them as soon as they entered the restaurant, and he looked at them both, from one to the other, like he was expecting bad news. "What's going on?"

"Nothing serious." Nikki laughed nervously. "Amy wants a job. There's none at the other restaurant, so we were wondering if..."

"Absolutely," Paul said with relief. "You scared me for a minute."

"Really? You have an opening?" Amy asked excitedly.

"I do. This is a very busy time of year, and I was considering hiring another server, so today is your lucky day," he beamed.

"Thank you," Amy gushed.

"No problem," he told her.

"What do I do? Is there like an interview or something?"

"We just had it." Paul laughed. "I already know you know how to wait tables. Here, let me introduce you to the maître d. He'll show you around."

"Okay," Amy replied as Paul took her over to the gentleman who led her off.

It was Nikki's turn to feel trepidation as Paul returned. "Look, Paul, about earlier. I didn't mean to snap at you. I was just a little overwhelmed..."

"And jealous?" he added.

She smiled weakly. "And jealous. I wanted to be the one to get through to her, but I guess it makes more sense that you did. You have a daughter, so you can relate."

"Nikki, there's no need to feel like that. You know I'm just helping."

"I know, which is why I feel stupid, so I apologize for it," she said and twiddled with her fingers. "In some way, I also felt like I was the reason she wanted to leave."

"You can't blame yourself for that. As you can see, she is her own person, and she still needs to process all of this."

"Yeah, you're right. Again." Nikki smiled. "What would I do without you?"

"You'd do just fine. You're a tough cookie."

Nikki laughed as Amy joined them again.

"You have a really nice place," she told Paul. "I'm looking forward to working here."

"Looking forward to having you." Paul smiled and patted her shoulder. "Welcome on board. I'll email your onboarding documents. Fill them out at your earliest convenience, and then we're good to go."

"I will," Amy replied.

"Now, if you'll both excuse me, I have to return to the kitchen."

"No problem. We'll talk later," Nikki said, and they walked out.

Amy was like a kid when they were in the car and

headed back to the Nestled Inn. She couldn't stop talking about the place as she compared it to all the other diners she'd worked in.

"I've never worked in a place this classy before," she said nervously.

"Don't worry, you'll be alright," Nikki assured her.

As soon as she dropped Amy off at the house, she drove to the hospital. Like every other visit, she hoped for good news but was equally let down when she was told there was no change. Like all the other times before, she pulled up the chair next to Trish's bed and took her hand.

"So Amy's staying here after all," she said as tears formed in her eyes. "I was scared for a moment that I'd chase her off, and you'd never get to meet her. But Paul has been a godsend. He convinced her to stay, and I can't wait for you to meet her. She's so beautiful and full of life. She reminds me so much of you when you were her age," Nikki said as she laid her head against Trish's hip.

"You need to wake up," she told her sister. "A lot of people are depending on you, and I think you'd do a better job than me at this mothering thing. It's hard to mother a twenty-one-year-old." She laughed softly. "I need help, so wake up and help me."

She shifted her head to look at Trish, but nothing was different. The same annoying beeping reminded her that her sister was still alive and was also a constant reminder that she was still in a deep coma. She hoped she could hear her but knew how painful it might be for her to be hearing all that was going on but not able to communicate any.

She probably felt trapped in her own body.

And just the thought brought fresh tears to Nikki's eyes.

Chapter Seventeen

Two days later, Nikki was at the house cleaning when her phone rang. Amy had started working at the restaurant the same day they'd talked to Paul, and she had been very excited after only day one.

She wrinkled her brows when she heard the phone. It couldn't be time to get Amy already. Where had the time gone?

She wiped her hand across her brow, and her heart raced when she saw Paul's name. It was like getting a call from the principal of your child's school. "Paul?" she asked when she answered.

"I'm afraid I have a bit of bad news," he began, increasing Nikki's anxiety as her knees suddenly weakened.

"What?" she asked, dreading that Amy had taken off without saying anything to her.

"Remember that guy we saw with Amy when we went to Seattle?" he asked.

"Yeah," she replied. "She'd said it was a rude

customer complaining about the menu or something like that."

"That doesn't seem to be the case now," Paul told her.

"What do you mean? What's going on?" Nikki could feel the heat rising under the bandanna she wore.

"He showed up here, and it's pretty clear they know each other," Paul said.

"What? Why would she lie about something like that?" Nikki asked furiously.

"I don't know, but you can ask her when she gets there. I'm going to take her home now. She's pretty shaken up."

"Oh my God," Nikki exclaimed and sank onto the edge of the bed. "Okay, thanks, Paul."

The chores were instantly forgotten as she hurried downstairs to await their arrival. A lump formed in her throat when his truck pulled into the driveway, and she hurried onto the porch. Amy got out and walked, hugging herself like a victim of a crime.

Nikki put her arm around her and led her inside, but she didn't want to attack her with questions right away. She just wanted to be sure she was alright, so she led her into the living room, where she perched on the edge of the seat.

Paul shared a concerned look with Nikki before he took the armchair to Amy's right. Nikki eventually sat down on the sofa next to Amy.

"Are you okay?" she asked her.

Amy rocked and shook her head. She quickly brushed away a tear.

"What's going on?" Nikki asked as calmly as she could. "Who was that?"

"That was Jake Tapper," Amy replied with a shrewd

smile. "My ex-boyfriend. But you can't tell him that. He won't leave me alone."

Nikki remembered the name from Greg's report and became even more concerned.

"Why didn't you tell us that the last time?"

"Why? I didn't know you," Amy retorted.

"I guess," Nikki admitted. "Why is he here? What does he want?"

Amy sighed. "He just won't leave me alone. We were together for a while, but he is a hothead and such a douchebag. We fought all the time and broke up even more times than that. We got back together after a couple of those fights, but now, I'm just done, but he won't take no for an answer," she told them. "I don't know what to do."

"Well, first of all, what he's doing is criminal," Paul advised her. "You can file a police report. Get a restraining order. He tailed you all the way from Seattle and knew where to find you."

"It wouldn't be hard for someone like him to do that." Amy sighed. "He has money. His family is rich. He gets away with a lot of things because of that."

"That doesn't mean jack squat," Nikki fumed. "Did he hurt you?"

"Not really," Amy replied, almost like she was trying to defend his actions, though abusive toward her. "He roughed me up a couple of times. Grabbed my arm too tightly, you know? Stuff like that. Nothing serious."

Nikki wasn't convinced. "It usually starts out like nothing. A poke here. A jab there. Next thing you know, you have a broken arm and a concussion. Guys like that shouldn't be taken lightly."

"I know," Amy said. "There was a time when I used

to blame myself for it—like if I hadn't talked back to him, he wouldn't have been angry. Or maybe if I loved him, he would change. After a while, I realized it wasn't going to happen, and I needed to get out," she said, averting her eyes to stare at the floor. "That's when he told me that if he can't have me, no one will."

Nikki gasped and covered her mouth. "Amy, that was a threat against your life! Oh my God!" Nikki got up and paced the floor as her anger intensified. "You can't go back to the restaurant."

Amy laughed incredulously. "You don't think he knows where I am now? Where to find me? He always does!" she said angrily. "It's like I can't get away from him, and it's been months of this. I can't take it anymore."

"You need to go to the police," Paul told her. "If there's no formal report, he can get away with anything. If anything should happen to you, God forbid, they'll want to know why you never said anything. They'll make you an accomplice after the fact."

Amy shook her head. "I know. I'm tired. Can I just go shower and get some sleep, please."

"Sure," Nikki said right away.

"Let me know if you need anything," Paul told her as he got up.

Amy walked upstairs while Nikki followed Paul to the door. "Thanks for looking out for her."

"I'm just glad I was there to see it happen," he told Nikki. "Don't let her sweep this under the rug. There are too many losers like that out there. You didn't take so long to find her for her to be taken by some jerk who can't let go."

"I know," Nikki said and hugged Paul. "Thanks for everything."

She was shaking and nervous after Paul left. She remembered what Amy had said—what if Jake was lurking outside? Suddenly, she didn't feel safe in her own home. She switched off the lights and walked upstairs.

Amy was in her bathrobe and sitting on the floor by the bed. Nikki stood in the doorway and leaned against the doorjamb.

"Please don't ask if I'm okay," Amy muttered.

"I wasn't going to say that," Nikki told her and walked over to sit next to her. "But have you ever said anything to anyone?"

"Like who?" she asked and wiped away fresh tears. "The girls think I'm stupid for letting someone like him get away. And my parents?" she asked and scoffed. "My father was the same."

"Oh no," Nikki replied sadly. "Did he hurt you?"

"Not me," she admitted. "But he would come home drunk many times and hit Mom," she recalled. "She never once called the cops. I was the one who did that, and many times, she accused me of wanting to break up the family. I didn't care, but he never stopped, and she never pressed charges. That's why I had to leave and why I never called the cops either. They don't do anything, and even if they tried, Jake's family would probably pay them to keep things quiet, and I would be slandered. I figured the best thing to do was to disappear."

"I'm so sorry you had to go through all that," Nikki said. "But is Jake one of the reasons you left Seattle?"

She nodded. "Yeah. I couldn't take it anymore, but I should have known better. That he would find me. He always did. Would you believe I told him I would call the cops on him, and he handed me his phone?"

"What?" Nikki asked with disdain.

"He knew nothing would come of it," Amy replied.

"Well, he just met his match," Nikki told her. "He's never going to bother you again. I'll make sure of it, and I'll start by making sure the cops know his name, even if he wants to bury it under money."

Amy sighed. "How did my life get to be like this?" she asked.

"I'm sorry, honey," Nikki said, and for the first time, she pulled her niece in for a warm embrace. "I can't tell you why these things happen, but I can promise things will get better."

"You know what's worse?" Amy asked as she pulled away.

"What?"

"He's here, so does that mean I should stay locked up in the house? I can't go to work. I can't go down to the beach. None of those things without looking over my shoulder?"

"No!" Nikki told her. "He won't steal your life from you. First thing tomorrow morning, we will make this right. And let's see how well Jake Tapper and his family will do when this hits the press."

"The press?" Amy asked with confusion.

"That's right. It's what I do. I'm an investigative jour-nalist, and my father made a career on people like those. No celebrity or wealthy family wants an irresponsible son dragging their name through the dirt. I might have to make a call to his family and see how they handle it, but either way, this nightmare is coming to an end. You can take my word for that," she said and got up. She stretched out her hand for Amy. "Come on, go take a shower and get some sleep."

Amy got up. "Thank you," she said and flew into Nikki's arms.

"It's going to be alright," Nikki told her as warm emotions flooded her. "In fact, I have an idea if you want to keep working."

"What?" Amy asked as her eyes widened.

"If you want, you could work at the inn, just so I can keep an eye on you."

"Doing what?" Amy asked.

"Doesn't matter. I'll find something for you to keep you occupied until this thing blows over."

Amy thought about it for a second. "I guess it's better than nothing."

"What do you mean better than nothing?" Nikki laughed. "There's work to go around. Not as glamorous as Lot 28 restaurant, but you could learn to love it."

"We'll see." Amy grinned.

"Okay, go get some rest. I'm going to finish some work I have."

"Journalism work?"

"Yep," Nikki replied and walked toward the door. "The one thing I know how to do best."

She was almost in her room when she heard the bathroom door click as Amy entered it and locked it. She couldn't imagine how she must feel to constantly be suffering abuse at the hands of ingrates. She was almost happy that Trish wasn't around to know how much Amy had suffered growing up and how much it still followed her.

As soon as she got into her room, she pulled out her laptop and looked up the Tappers. Amy hadn't been kidding—they were loaded and seemed to have a hand in every charitable donation and school funding in Seattle.

They would be a tough crowd, but she reveled in a challenge.

She pulled her hair back into a ponytail and began surfing for information. She'd do her due diligence first, but the one thing she was sure of was that Jake Tapper had harassed her niece for the last time.

His family would pay, and she was the one who would bring them to their knees.

Chapter Eighteen

The following morning, Nikki called Paul, and they met up along a trail by the seaside.

It was a beautiful morning, and the pinkish hues from the rising sun still colored the horizon. The trail was raised, so it was like being on a cliff, and Nikki and Paul sat on the bench overlooking one of Nature's glorious wonders in the crashing waves.

"Why did you have us meet out here?" he asked.

"I don't want Amy to know about this, but I think I should hire Greg to find out more about Jake," Nikki began. "Last night, I tried to find dirt on them on the web, but there wasn't as much as a dirty sock to be found."

"I'm not surprised," Paul replied. "There's a lot you can hide under money."

"What do you think about hiring Greg?" she asked anxiously.

"I'm all in," he stated. "He needs to learn a lesson. I'll call him for you and see how soon he can get started."

"Thanks," Nikki told him. "I just can't believe all that

she has been through. First with her abusive father and now with the boyfriend."

"I'm glad Trish isn't around." Paul chuckled. "She would have gone loose on that poor boy."

"Nothing poor about that boy, but I had the same idea last night—that she would be hurting so much to know about everything that Amy had to endure all those years that we weren't in her life."

"It's good that she doesn't, then," Paul replied. "But let me get on this and get back to you."

"Okay," Nikki replied as they got up and left.

It didn't take long for Greg to work his magic. The trio met a few days later at the same bench on the trail overlooking the sea.

"You're not going to like this," Greg began as he pulled out a file. "I wish I'd dug a little deeper the first time, but that boy has always been trouble."

"What now?" Nikki asked as she took the reports from Greg, and she and Paul looked them over.

"He's been in all sorts of trouble over his lifetime, and this isn't the first time he has harassed a former girlfriend either."

"Shocker," Paul replied sarcastically.

"Yeah, shocker," Greg agreed. "Anyway, he got a little too handsy before, and the young woman, Michelle Maddix, had to file a restraining order against him. Of course, he couldn't keep away. He stalked her continuously and openly, a clear violation of the restraining order. He was arrested, but then he got off with a warning. A slap on the wrist really. Again, shocker," Greg said and shook his head in disbelief. "You'd be surprised how common this kind of thing is."

"I can," Nikki replied. "I've seen my share of gossip at

my father's hands and twenty years of my own. What else?" Nikki asked as she flipped the pages.

"Well, he was warned that if he appeared before the courts again, they wouldn't be so lenient next time. He would be charged to the full extent of the law and serve hard time."

"It would serve him right," Nikki replied bitterly. "He can't continue to prey on young girls, destroy their self-esteem and damage them emotionally, and then move on to the next. He can't get away with it."

"You need to get her to press charges and take out a restraining order against him. She's the only one who can."

"I don't see why she wouldn't," Nikki said.

Greg glanced over at her. "Victims often blame themselves and rarely do what needs to be done. Make sure she does."

"I will," Nikki told him. "Thanks for the great work again."

Greg got up and left, and at that time, Nikki asked Paul to be there when she told Amy the truth.

It didn't go over the way Nikki saw it in her head. Amy seemed to have been familiar with the information they presented to her.

"What now?" she asked after Nikki had told her all about the other offenses Jake had committed.

"You need to make a report and file for a restraining order," Nikki told her.

Amy got up and raked her hair backward. "Do I really need to do that?" she asked. "I mean, Paul roughed him up pretty good at the restaurant. I think he got the message."

"Has he ever gotten the message before?" Nikki asked almost angrily.

"No, but that's because no one has ever stood up to him," she explained. "No one's seen him around town since then."

"How would you know? He's always been good at sneaking around," Nikki snapped, and Paul gave her a warning look. "Look, I don't mean to come down on you, but this boy has abused you, and abuse like that doesn't just go away. Even if you won't do something for yourself, do it for the next girl he will prey on because there's always another."

"I don't know," Amy replied. "I don't want to mess up his life."

"You're not the one doing that," Nikki said as she stood before Amy. "He's the one making a mess of his life and that of others. Why can't you see that?"

"I don't want to go to the cops, okay?" she said and stormed off.

Nikki was flabbergasted as she watched Amy stomping up the stairs. "This is unbelievable. Why is she protecting him?"

"I don't know," Paul replied. "But maybe it's like Greg said, the victims always feel responsible somehow. I just think it's important that you not let her forget."

"You can be sure I won't," Nikki replied as she stormed off and headed for the Nestled Inn. She was fuming so much she could barely see the person in front of her, and she almost collided with Nelly as the old woman entered the lobby.

"Oh, I'm so sorry," Nikki gushed.

"That's okay." Nelly laughed. "I'm still standing."

Then her eyes narrowed on Nikki. "What's wrong? You're upset."

Nikki sighed and wiped her hand down her face. "I just have a lot going on."

"Come. Sit with me and tell me what's going on with you," Nelly said and hobbled off.

Nikki followed her, feeling the need to offload and not be rude at the same time. They sat in one of the loveseats along the wall in the lobby area. Nelly waited patiently for Nikki to speak.

"It's just that my niece had this boyfriend who's been harassing her because she broke up with him. She's not the first girl he's done this to, and she knows it, but she refuses to file a report or a restraining order. I don't get how she can't see how dangerous this guy is. He needs to be locked up. And that's not even what I'm asking her to do. But he's been stalking her for months. That's why she showed up here. What's it going to take for her to see who he is and what he's capable of?"

"Oh, I see," Nelly replied. "Did she love this boyfriend?"

"I don't know," Nikki replied honestly. She'd never thought to ask.

"Was there any other kind of abuse in her life before him?" the old woman asked wisely.

"Her adoptive father used to abuse her mother, and she was forced to call the cops on him several times."

"I think I'm beginning to see the picture now," Nelly remarked. "Her biological mother abandoned her. Her adoptive parents abused her, and now her boyfriend, possibly someone she used to love. She doesn't trust anyone, and certainly not an aunt who just showed up in her life. Everyone she should be close to has abused her or left her. She feels alone and thinks she's better off on her own."

Nikki sighed. "But if that's the case, what do I do?"

"You can't do anything but support her and hope she comes around. All of this has to make sense in her mind, or she will end up in the same cycle over and over again. She must conquer this demon herself."

Just then, Kaylyn motioned Nikki over, and she excused herself and thanked Nelly for her encouragement. Her words never left Nikki that day, but she already knew that she couldn't force Amy to make a choice. All she could do was present the facts to her.

* * *

Over the next few days, Amy was more like her usual self, and it was as if Jake never existed. Nikki let her guard down and allowed her to go down to the beach with some newly made friends. Amy had just returned from one such excursion while Nikki was upstairs finishing up an investigative piece.

"Amy, is that you?" she called when she heard the front door open. No answer came. "Amy?"

Just then she heard a loud thud, and then something crashed to the floor. She tossed her laptop aside and crept to the edge of the stairs. "Amy? Is that you?" she asked as her heart pounded.

Still, no answer came, and the hair on the back of Nikki's neck stood.

"Release my arm!" Amy cried.

When Nikki reached the bottom of the stairs, she saw the front door open, but no Amy.

"Let me go!"

Nikki's head snapped to the right when she realized Amy's voice was coming from the kitchen. She moved closer, inching along the wall, and peeked around the corner. That was when she saw Jake rough handling Amy. Anger spurned inside Nikki, and she made a mad dash for the supplies closet, where she grabbed a baseball bat she knew was tucked away inside. She dialed 911 and left the line open so they could hear before placing the phone on the mantel.

Amy was still struggling against Jake when she returned, and she appeared in the kitchen doorway just as he lifted his hand to strike Amy.

Nikki positioned the bat in her hand. "If you bring that hand down on my niece, it's the last thing that hand will touch!" she said in a deathly calm voice that would chill even a ghost.

"You need to stay out of this," Jake warned her.

That didn't help his cause. Nikki moved closer. "I'm going to say this one more time. Let go of my niece and leave now if you still want that hand!"

Jake held her stare and then started backing away. "This isn't over!" he said as he pointed threateningly at Amy.

"Just go! I called the cops, and I'm sure you don't want them here."

He got nervous upon hearing that, and he turned on his heels and prepared to run when he collided with Paul's steel chest.

"What's going on here?" Paul asked, just as Amy ran from the kitchen and into Nikki's arms. The bat fell from her hand as she hugged Amy.

"He attacked her," Nikki told Paul.

A dark cloud shadowed his face as he collared the boy moments before the sound of sirens filled the air.

"Not this time," Paul snarled at Jake, and Sarah, who'd come over for a visit, stepped aside so Paul could drag Jake outside.

The cops came, took a report from everyone, and handcuffed Jake. Considering he would be a repeat offender, Nikki hoped they would lock him away for good.

"This is not what I expected to find when Sarah and I left the house," Paul told Nikki.

"Let me see your arm," the nurse in Sarah spoke up as she hurried over to Amy. She examined her for bruises and realized she had a few from Jake's earlier abuse. Her left eye had already begun to swell, and Nikki's heart seized in her chest when she realized how much she had just endured. "You'll need to get some ice on that, and when you're feeling better, I can go with you to the hospital. Would you like that?"

Amy nodded in agreement. Tears continued to roll down her face, and Sarah leaned in and hugged her. "Shh," she hushed her. "It's okay now. It's over. No one's going to hurt you again."

Amy cried even more, and after a couple of seconds, there were no dry eyes near them.

"I can't believe I was so stupid," Amy said as she cursed herself. "I should have listened to Nikki and Paul and had him locked away."

"There's no need to go backward now," Sarah told her. "He's locked up now, and you'll get better. Stronger even. I can tell."

Sarah's kind eyes were all that Amy needed, and in an instant, the two connected on a deep level.

"Now, how about we get you cleaned up and pretty again, huh?" Sarah asked. "Maybe we can play some online games where we get to beat up some boys."

Amy laughed despite her situation. "I like that idea."

"Okay, come on," Sarah said.

Paul and Nikki looked on like spectators at the two young women, and Paul marveled at how much his daughter had grown.

"That was the introduction, by the way." He laughed. "Now you've met my Sarah."

"She's incredible, Paul," Nikki congratulated him. "You raised a good kid."

"It was mostly God, but I'll accept on his behalf." He smiled.

Nikki laughed. "Come on. I think we need to find a way to occupy our time. How about we cook?"

"Together? We haven't done that in a long time," Paul beamed.

"No time like the present," Nikki said as she looped her arm through his and led him to the kitchen.

151

Chapter Nineteen

Things were sort of sketchy following the incident with Jake, but as time passed, Amy was less shaken by the incident.

Maybe there was comfort in the fact that Jake was locked up, and he would finally be out of her life for good this time.

Amy was in the kitchen making breakfast when Nikki walked in. "I thought you said you wanted to be a pastry chef," she teased when she noticed the breakfast sausages, the bologna, and the waffles.

"I do, but we can't live off pastry," Amy beamed. "I thought I'd treat you for once even though I'm sure this is nothing like the biscuits or muffins you make."

Nikki laughed. "I had a lot more practice, but you, my dear, will be under the tutelage of a great pastry chef."

"Oh my God, do you know how amazing that is." Amy grinned. "I can't wait. One day, my name will be on one of the most amazing bakeries in Camano, or Seattle, or wherever. I will be the Gordon Ramsay of baking."

Nikki laughed as she watched her niece, who was

filled with hope for the future. "I'm glad to see you like this."

"Yeah," Amy replied and handed her aunt a plate. She joined her by the breakfast counter, but Nikki could see that even though she had prepared the meal, she didn't have an appetite for it.

"It's a bad sign when the chef won't eat their own food," Nikki teased. "Should I be worried?"

Amy laughed weakly. "Not this time."

"What's eating you?" Nikki asked her as she bit into a sausage.

"I want to go visit her," Amy said softly.

"Trish?" Nikki asked as her heart quickly filled with joy.

"Yeah," Amy replied. "I need to."

"Absolutely," Nikki said as she covered Amy's palm with her own. "You're making me so happy right now." Nikki brushed tears away.

"At least now I know why I cry so much." Amy laughed. "Must be in the genes."

Nikki shrugged. "Must be, and maybe from Mom."

"When can we go?" Amy asked.

"She's in a private room, so we can go whenever you like."

"How about this morning, then?"

"Great!" Nikki beamed.

She might as well have been gliding to the hospital with Amy. Her heart was full to bursting, and the only missing factor was an awakened Trish. She needed to see her daughter, but for the moment, Nikki was just glad that Amy had agreed to go see her.

A somber mood greeted them as they walked into the room, and Nikki heard Amy gasp. She understood well what she must be feeling because similar emotions had overwhelmed her when she saw how Trish was strung up and seemed on the verge of death.

Amy walked gingerly over to her, and every few steps or so, she turned to look back at Nikki, who came up alongside her.

"Hey, Trish," Nikki spoke first. "I have someone I'd like you to meet," she said and paused before she looked at Amy. "Go ahead."

Amy visibly shook as she took Trish's pale and frail hand in hers. "She's so thin," she commented.

"I know," Nikki replied. "A shadow of the vibrant woman I know."

Nikki pulled up two chairs, and they both sat. Amy didn't release Trish's hand, and eventually, she covered it with her other hand.

"I'm Amy, your daughter," she began. "I didn't know about you until a few weeks ago, but I wish I had known you sooner. Life, huh? Just as soon as you start looking for me, life said no, and here we are." She sighed. "It's kind of messed up, isn't it? But I'm still hoping you wake up, and I get to see you and talk with you. If you're anything like Nikki, I know you're awesome," she continued.

Nikki tensed as she listened to Amy's heartfelt words to her mother and placed her arm around her for support. "I'm going outside for some water."

Amy nodded as Nikki left the two of them alone so she could have some privacy. She was in the waiting area, flipping through old magazines, when Amy emerged.

"I thought you were going to come back," she said.

"I felt you needed some time alone, especially on your first visit," Nikki said. "Are you done with the visit?"

"For now." Amy smiled. "I'll be back."

They both walked out of the hospital, and Amy turned to Nikki as the car pulled into traffic. "Is it weird that I feel like she heard me?"

"Nope," Nikki said. "That's the same way I feel all the time I'm with her, and I refuse to believe it's just wishful thinking. But when she wakes up, we can ask her for sure."

Amy smiled. "Maybe it will be like a dream that fades when you wake up, so she won't be able to tell anyway."

"Maybe," Nikki agreed.

The two grew closer as the days rolled by, and with Jake locked up, Amy resumed her job at Lot 28 as a server.

But that wasn't enough for Nikki. One day when she got home, she confronted Amy. "I know you had an issue with this the last time, but what do you think about pressing charges against Jake once and for all and getting that restraining order?"

Amy sighed. "That didn't do anything the last time with that other girl."

"That time, he was a new offender. He got away with a warning. He's now back with the same thing. He won't get off so easily this time, and if they try, I will put them on blast for it."

Amy laughed at her aunt using modern lingo. "I bet you would, but I think it's what's best. I've already given them a report of the incident. Now, I need to make it formal. I hate police stations," she admitted. "There's something so sinister about them to me."

"They're meant to serve and to protect," Nikki told her.

"I know, but the ones I met neither served nor protected," Amy declared.

"That's not all of them," Nikki reminded her. "Some of them care deeply about their jobs."

"I guess." Amy sighed. "Either way, I just want this behind me."

"I couldn't agree more." They visited the precinct that afternoon, and Amy pressed charges against Jake. She would have to wait for a court date to obtain a restraining order, but she wasn't in a hurry with him locked up.

"How about we go shopping?" Nikki asked when they left. "We haven't done anything girly since you've been here."

"I can definitely do that," Amy replied excitedly. "You're buying, right?"

Nikki laughed. "Yes, I'm buying. What are aunts for?"

They drove to the coast, where kiosks littered the beachfront. Vendors sold potted items, collectibles, keepsakes, T-shirts, jewelry, and household crafts. Nikki and Amy weaved their way through the throng of people searching for interesting pieces for their homes or persons.

They stopped by a kiosk that had pottery pieces, and Nikki picked up a beautifully painted jar that would make a nice attraction over the fireplace. "I love this," she told Amy, who was busy looking at charm bracelets behind her.

"I like these," she beamed, then noticed the jar in Nikki's hand. "That looks nice too."

"So believable," Nikki teased.

"No, I really mean it." Amy giggled. "Where's the other one?"

Nikki gasped. "You're right. Two would look better. Hmm," she mused. "Maybe I'll just find a place where one works."

They continued checking out the stalls, picking up pieces as they went, until they wound up at The Oar, a pub and finger-food joint.

"I'm starving," Amy said as she slid into the booth seat.

The air was rich with the charred smell of meat on a spit or roasted over an open fire. They salivated as they waited for the baby back ribs that they ordered, and in minutes, their hands and faces were sticky messes of grease and sauce.

"Does everything taste good on this island?" Amy asked.

"You've never been here?" Nikki asked in shock.

"Yeah, like on a day trip, and we'd have our own food and stuff, but now that I'm tasting the local food, I'm blown away."

"I'm glad you like it." Nikki smiled as she wiped the napkin across her mouth. "Maybe you'll consider moving here for good."

"I thought I was already here," Amy said and winked. "How about you? I know you lived in Arlington. Is Camano now your home for good?"

Nikki smiled as she considered it. Back in Arlington, she had her job, but that was about it. And she had a job she could take anywhere. Camano represented a family she had always craved for but never had the opportunity to have and to reunite with a sister who had been estranged for so long. It was a pleasant prospect in her mind's eye, and she definitely would consider moving.

"It could be." She laughed.

"It better be. I could love it here," Amy observed. "Good food, the ocean, great friends. I've only just met Sarah, but I can already tell we're going to be great friends. She invited me over for the weekend. She said we could do some outdoor stuff—whatever is happening this weekend."

"That's great," Nikki said. "You're already planting your roots. When we were kids, our parents used to rent a summer home here every year."

"No kidding," Amy exclaimed.

"Yep," Nikki told her. "We practically grew up here. I just moved away because I was so hurt and bitter."

"Maybe it's time that you moved back. Speaking of which, what's going on between you and Paul?"

It was Nikki's turn to blush. "What do you mean? Nothing's going on."

"Exactly," Amy said. "And why is that? You two had a thing back in the day. He's single. You're single. He's attractive. You know, for a guy his age."

Nikki laughed. "A guy his age."

"You know what I mean." Amy giggled. "We could all be one big happy family. And I think he's still into you."

"Oh stop." Nikki blushed.

"Trust me, I know these things." Amy grinned. "He wants you."

"Stop making me think about him like that," Nikki told her.

"I won't," Amy said and leaned forward. "Not until you both agree to go out on a date."

"I don't think now's the best time for that," Nikki said.

"It never is," Amy pressed. "I'm not going to let up. You're going to have to just let me win."

And Nikki could tell she wasn't joking, but the more she was forced to think about Paul, the more she wondered if it would be Amy who was winning.

Or her!

Chapter Twenty

"*No! Mom, please do something.*" *Nikki knelt before her mother, her face tearstained and her eyes pleading for help.*

Her mother, who had chosen to stare at the wall all along instead of her daughter, finally turned to look at her.

Nikki pulled back from the angry determination in the woman's stormy blue eyes. "You are the reason she is in this position in the first place, Nikki. Why would I help you to further mess up her life? After all the work your father has put in to ensure that she stays the course."

"Mom..." Nikki looked at her mother, flabbergasted. Sophia had never spoken to her in such a way before. She'd never agreed with Stewart's schemes but had instead always made it seem like she had no choice but to side with him.

But now...

Nikki couldn't understand where the venom directed at her was coming from. She was completely floored.

"It's all your fault, Nikki. If you hadn't chosen to run off and marry that man..." Sophia shook her head, the

contempt with which she spoke about Josh telling. Sophia focused her stare on her daughter once more. "You are a bad influence on your sister. She only did what she did because she emulated you so much. You destroyed her future—"

"No! That's not true," Nikki refuted, her neck swinging her head vigorously from side to side.

"Listen to your mother. She is right. This is all your fault."

Nikki swiveled on her heels to look up at the man staring down at her, his own eyes filled with accusation and disappointment.

"I had so many plans for you, but you have shown that you cannot be trusted. I won't allow you to destroy your sister's life any more than you have."

His biting threat caused Nikki's heart to pump wildly. Her eyes swung frantically to her sister, who stood by his side with her eyes downcast.

"Trish...don't let him do this to you...to us," Nikki pleaded softly.

Trish's chin slowly came up until her tear-filled, guilt-ridden face became visible. "I'm sorry, Nikki...I...I can't," she responded, her voice cracking with pain.

Nikki felt like her heart had shattered into a million tiny shards, but before she could dwell on it too much, the setting changed, and she was standing in the foyer of the B & B. She spotted Amy heading away from the reception desk toward her, a broad smile on her face.

"You ready to go?"

"Go where?" Nikki asked, confused by the turn of events.

"To the movies. We planned to spend time together. Remember?" Amy responded, giving her a weird look.

"Right. I'm sorry I just got a little confused." Nikki smiled.

"No worries," Amy reassured her before holding her arm out for her to take it. Nikki eagerly hooked their arms, and they turned to walk out the door. Only in the doorway stood her parents, arms folded across their chests.

"What are you doing here now?" she asked, stepping in front of Amy as if to hide her from them.

"We're here for our granddaughter," her father responded without delay.

"You can't be serious," Nikki returned, stepping even farther in front of the young woman.

"What's going on?" her niece asked from behind her, her voice filled with curiosity.

"Amy, sweetheart, we're your grandparents. We're here to take you back to Seattle with us to be a family, to live the life you deserved all along." Her mother tried to look over her shoulder at Amy as she spoke, a welcoming smile on her lips.

Nikki scoffed. "Are you serious?" Automatically, her arms came up to fold over her chest. "After all these years and after all you did to Trish and me, why do you think you deserve to just come waltz into her life as if you aren't the reason she grew up away from this family?" she asked pointedly.

Silence ensued. Nikki was certain the erratic beating of her heart could be heard unaided.

"Why do you think you have a say in her life?" Her father spoke this time. Stewart's deep blue eyes narrowed at her. "She's not your daughter. I seem to recall that you can't have children, and Trish didn't agree to give her to you."

Nikki's blunt nails somehow found a way to dig deeply

into the flesh of her arms as the force of her father's words almost bowled her over. All the pain from twenty-one years ago seeped into her like water filling a dam. Stewart and Sophia stalked toward her, and before she could process what was happening, they pulled Amy out from behind her and toward them. Finally shaking out of her daze, she reached for her niece's free arm and held it firmly, halting them from pulling her farther.

"No," she said firmly. "You are not talking to her."

Her father's eyes blazed with anger as his face reddened, but just as before, everything changed without warning, and instead of Stewart, it was Jake holding on to Amy.

"Let go," he said in a threatening voice to Amy.

"No," Nikki spoke firmly.

"All right," he said as if he was giving up, but then a sinister smile turned up his lips and his crazed eyes made him look like one of the monsters from a horror movie. "If I can't have her, no one can." He reached his free hand into his pocket.

Nikki braced herself to fight for her niece but became distracted by the sniffling sounds coming from behind her. She took her eyes off Jake to look back at her sister. She was still pretty banged up, and she was also attached to the machines that had been keeping her alive. Still, she was sitting up in the hospital bed, and countless sobs shook her frame.

"Please. Don't let them take away my baby."

Nikki woke up with a start. She propped herself up by her elbows and looked around the semi-dark room in confusion. She pulled herself farther up in bed until her back rested against the headboard. That had been an intense and frightening dream. She could still feel her heart racing in her chest. She turned her head to the side and noticed that the digital clock read 2:32 a.m.

After a good two minutes of calming herself, she threw her legs over the edge of the bed and stood. She needed to go check on Amy.

When she made it to the door at the end of the hall, she noticed light streaming from under it. "Amy, are you awake?" She knocked.

There was some rustling before the door swung open to reveal Amy with dark circles under her eyes.

"Are you alright?"

"Yeah. I am," Amy replied, with the faintest of movement of her lips upward.

Nikki wasn't convinced. Amy moved aside and allowed her to enter the room before closing the door with a soft thud. She walked over to her bed and sat, folding her legs under her.

Nikki stood for a little while, studying her before she took a seat on the bed.

"What's wrong?" she finally asked, turning her head to look at Amy.

Amy's shoulders went up to her ears before settling back in their normal position. "I can't sleep," she said, turning her head to give Nikki a sheepish look before facing forward once more.

Nikki swiveled her upper half and rested her palm flat on the bed to balance herself as she faced Amy fully. She canvassed the younger woman's side profile, noting her furrowed brow and folded lips. A deep seat of concern made her chest heavy. "Is it because of Jake?"

Amy shook her head in a swift no. Nikki waited. After prolonged silence, Amy breathed in deeply and slowly released it, her shoulders being directed by the rise and fall of her chest.

"I keep having this feeling that none of this will last... that probably none of it is even real," she confessed, making wide gestures with her arms before they fell by her side. "It's like I'm waiting for the other shoe to drop, for all of this to finally disappear, and then I'll wake up and realize that this was all just a dream."

Nikki wanted to rush in to reassure her that her feelings weren't true. She wanted to make her understand that it all would last, but she also knew Amy had more to say, so she remained silent.

Amy released another deep sigh, her shoulders sagging like one beaten down.

"I keep...waiting for this newfound family and the love you already have for me to just..." Her eyes shone with her vulnerability as they cut to Nikki. "I'm waiting for it to be too good to be true so that I can go back to the crappy life I've always known," she said plainly.

"Amy, listen to me. There is no way you're ever getting rid of me or your mother when she wakes up. We...I have loved you all your life. I have wanted you from the moment I found out Trish was pregnant with you," Nikki spoke with feeling. She raised her hand to rest it on her niece's cheek lovingly. "Even though we didn't get to witness you growing up all these years, we are going to spend the rest of our lives loving you and making up for lost time." Nikki looked at her niece with what she could only hope was convincing enough as she finished. "You better get used to it, sweetie, because you're stuck with me...and your mother."

Amy's face relaxed into a smile, and that was enough for Nikki to pull her fully into her arms. She hugged her tight and whispered against her temple, "I'm so happy we found you."

"Me too," Amy replied.

After a few minutes, the two finally separated. "Wanna have some hot chocolate in the kitchen with me?" Nikki offered.

"Yeah. Sure," Amy accepted, sliding off the bed with her. The two made their way to the kitchen, and Amy sat at the island watching her aunt prepare their hot beverage.

"What are you planning for your future? Where do you see yourself in, say, five or ten years from now?" Nikki brought the steaming liquid to her lips and took a sip, watching her niece contemplate her response across from her. Her hands enveloped the mug as she stared into the dark, opaque liquid.

"Well, for starters, I want to go to culinary school to become a pastry chef like I told you. I've been saving all the money and tips that I can from my job to pay for it."

Nikki bobbed her head in understanding. "And after that?" she prodded.

Amy looked up at her aunt, determination on her face. "I want to own my own pastry shop," she revealed.

"That is a wonderful idea, Amy. I think you would be an excellent pastry chef. You're already so talented," she cheered. "I mean, your key lime pie is already a heavenly treat, and I'm still waiting to taste that strawberry short-cake you promised to make."

Amy giggled at the face her aunt made talking about her cakes.

"You have a gift, Amy, and any culinary school would be excited to offer you a spot. All you need to do now is send out the applications. I'll help you."

Amy smiled gratefully. "Thanks. I really appreciate that."

Nikki returned her smile. "I know Paul would be very happy to help you, you know. Give you a few pointers while you wait for your acceptance. Who knows? Maybe when you're finished, he would consider adding a pastry chef to his kitchen rotation...Just until you're ready to venture out on your own."

Amy nodded as she listened. A smirk graced her lips, and the mischievous glint in her eyes made Nikki cut what she was about to say.

"What?" she asked.

"I was just thinking it's cute how much you depend on Paul even though you guys aren't dating or anything," Amy replied innocently, then took a sip of her hot chocolate.

"That's because he's my friend and a nice person," Nikki managed to say.

"Are you sure there's nothing more to it?" Amy pressed, the knowing smile tipping her lips further upward. "Because it sure feels to me that you both are harboring fee—"

"Okay. We're not having this conversation. It's late, and I'm going back to sleep," Nikki interrupted. She was sure her cheeks were red by now and as clear as day to Amy.

"Oh, come on. I know you must have some idea that he likes you," Amy pressed, making air quotes at the latter part of her statement.

"Nuh-uh. We are not doing this," Nikki returned, then stood to her feet. "Time for bed, young lady."

"But..."

"No buts," she said, raising her hands and shooing Amy toward the door.

"Oh man! You're no fun." Amy pouted as she left the kitchen before her.

"Love you!" Nikki called after her with a grin.

Chapter Twenty-One

Nikki woke up feeling more relaxed than she had in days. She pulled herself up until her back rested against the plush but firmly upholstered headboard. Her mind flashed to the conversation she'd had with Amy a few hours ago, and a broad smile lit up her face.

Whatever barrier had remained between them was now completely broken or almost—she had felt it. Amy had willingly confided her fears to her, and Nikki was certain that she had heard her when she promised she'd never leave her no matter what. The smile that had broken out on the young woman's face and the way the conversation turned out gave Nikki assurance.

"Trish, I wish you could see what a remarkable young woman your daughter is," she spoke wistfully before throwing off the thin cotton sheets. She swung her legs over the edge of the bed and stood to her feet. After a few languid stretches, she headed for the bathroom for a well-desired shower.

"Mmm. It smells great in here," Nikki praised as the

aroma of cinnamon, vanilla, nutmeg, and other spices from the freshly baked pastry infiltrated her nostrils as she stepped into the kitchen. The rich aroma of the dark roast and the smell of bacon also wafted to her nose and caused her mouth to salivate as her tummy rumbled with need.

Amy looked up from loosening the muffins from the sides of the pan with a smile that rivaled the sun. "I thought, since I'm about to go to culinary school, why not get in as much practice as I can, and what better way to do that than to feed my favorite aunt all of my special recipes?"

"I'm your only aunt." Nikki chuckled, walking farther into the kitchen and taking in the spread before her. "If this is what I should look forward to regularly, pretty soon, I won't be able to make it downstairs."

"Oh, this isn't all for you. I thought we could offer the guests at the inn the muffins and cinnamon rolls for feedback," Amy explained.

Nikki's head tipped forward in thought. "That's a great idea. Having a wider test audience would be good," she agreed. "Not before I've had my own taste testing, though," she added, pulling out one of the stools and sitting at the island.

When Amy finished packaging the pastries for the Nestled Inn, the two sat and ate. Nikki couldn't stop gushing. Everything she ate was quite delectable. She liked the way the muffin tasted—not too sweet and just the right amount of blueberries and nuts—and it melted against her tongue like butter after a few chews.

"There is no doubt about it. You've outdone yourself this time. If you decided to open that shop right now, you would always be guaranteed a customer," Nikki praised, taking another bite from the muffin.

"Thanks. I really appreciate that," Amy returned, her face breaking out in a smile.

Just then, Nikki felt something soft and furry rub against her leg. She looked down to see Tabby's glassy, yellow eyes staring back at her.

Meow.

"I'm guessing you want something to fill your tummy too, don't you?" Nikki smiled, reaching down to scratch behind her ear. The cat purred in pleasure.

Pushing away from the island, she went into the bottom cupboard drawer and came out with two stainless steel bowls. Tabby wrapped her lithe frame around Nikki's ankle as her calls became more frantic.

Nikki placed a good serving of cat food in one bowl before pouring water in the other and setting them down for Tabby. The cat eagerly dashed to the dish and began eating.

"You've really grown attached to that cat," Amy noted as she stood moving dirty dishes to the sink.

"That would suck because I have to take her back to the shelter so that they can find her a home," Nikki replied, straightening up.

"Oh," Amy replied, surprised. "I thought you were already planning to keep her."

"I would love to, but I'm not sure I can. Not right now."

Amy nodded in understanding.

"I should take her back to the Humane Society. I also have something to discuss with Reed..." Nikki's brows furrowed in thought before her eyes brightened with an idea. "Why don't you come with me? They're putting on an event to support and show appreciation for your mother. I need to meet with her friend Reed, and I could use your input on things."

"Okay. I would love to," her niece readily agreed.

After cleaning the kitchen and dropping the muffins and cinnamon rolls off at the inn, Nikki drove them to the Humane Society.

"Nikki, I'm so glad you came. We have a few more things to finalize for the fundraising," Reed greeted her with a smile.

"Hi, Reed," she greeted back, taking the hand he offered in a warm handshake. "I had a few things that I wanted to discuss with you too," she said as they separated. She noticed his eyes zeroed in on something behind her, and his brows furrowed as his lips parted in what could only be described as shock.

"Oh. This is Amy, Trish's daughter," she said, stepping aside to give him a better look at her.

"Hi." Amy waved shyly.

"Hi. It's a pleasure to meet you," Reed said, holding out his hand for her to take. "Your mother would be over the moon if she could see you now." A dark shadow passed over his face before he pasted on a smile.

Amy gave him a partial smile as she released his hand.

"I discussed it with the other committee members, and we all agreed that it would be a good idea if this event becomes a yearly fundraiser in honor of Trish, and the funds would go to someone who had an accident and isn't able to take care of their medical expenses."

"That's a great idea, Reed. Trish will love it," Nikki said appreciatively.

Reed smiled in agreement before launching into the other fundraising details.

Amy, who had been walking the grounds, came up to them. "I'm gonna go in a bit. I promised Sarah that I'd meet her and Aaron for lunch at Lot 28," she excused herself.

"Do you want me to take you?" Nikki asked with concern.

"No, it's fine. They're picking me up on their way over there," Amy reassured her.

"Okay," Nikki responded, relieved. Just then, the honking of a car horn caught their attention.

"Gotta go. Bye."

"She is really a lovely young woman," Reed complimented, bringing Nikki's attention away from her niece's retreating back.

"That she is." Nikki smiled proudly. "About the cat..." she said, launching into another topic of discussion.

"Oh yes. We have room for her now. You can bring her back when you're ready."

"I was actually thinking about keeping her. She's grown on me," Nikki revealed.

"Even better," he replied, pleased. "Let's get you some pet ownership forms to sign, and you can pick out a name tag for..."

"Tabby."

"For Tabby."

And just like that, Nikki was a cat owner.

* * *

Ding!

Nikki put down the book she had been reading, stood to her feet, and walked out of the living room. She managed to open the door after the second ring. Her heart rate quickened and her face automatically broke into a smile at the sight of Paul standing before her.

"Hi," she greeted, her voice coming out a little breathier than she'd intended.

"Hi," Paul returned, reaching over to envelop her in a hug. His musky cedarwood and allspice scent penetrated her senses. She caught herself before she snuggled closer to him and moved out of the embrace with a smile.

"I came by to check on the restaurant and thought I'd check on you too."

Nikki moved back, allowing him to enter, then closed the door and walked him to the living room. She excused herself to get them a cool drink of lemonade. After handing Paul a glass, she settled into the couch opposite the one he sat in. She watched as he put the glass to his lips and tipped his head backward as he took a long drink of the cold beverage. His Adam's apple bobbed with every gulp.

"I saw Sarah and Amy by Lot 28 having lunch on my way over here."

"How did she look?" Nikki asked, leaning forward in her seat.

"They were laughing about something when I was leaving," he responded. "Amy looks happy...comfortable. Sarah really likes her. She said that if she had a little sister, she would like her to be like Amy."

Nikki smiled broadly. "I'm really happy to hear that. She needs some positive influence in her life," she commented before her shoulders drooped and her brows furrowed in regret. "We weren't there for her when she needed us, and she had to grow up the way she did." Her eyes clouded over.

"After all of that, she deserves some good in her life.

She needs some good role models to help her heal from what her adoptive parents put her through...what that lowlife did to her." Her hands tightened on the armrests, causing her knuckles to go white at the vision of Jake holding her niece roughly with his other hand raised and ready to strike. She wished she had been able to do more to keep him away from Amy.

"I hope he stays in jail for a long time. He could rot for all I care," she spoke with much venom.

Paul's pursed lips and the look in his eyes made her uneasy. "What's wrong?"

"Jake is out on bail. His mother came to bail him out and left town with him as soon as he was released," he spoke regretfully.

Her heart hit the bottom of her chest. "What?" She stared at Paul with dread.

"I'm sorry, Nikki. There's nothing we can do about it until th—"

"No," she almost screamed as she launched herself out of the chair and began pacing the space before her. "I can't accept that there's nothing that can be done. I need to go see his mother and speak to her woman to woman... let her know she needs to keep that evil spawn away from Amy," she spoke frantically.

"Nikki." Paul sighed as he rested the glass on top of the coffee table. "I don't think that's such a good idea. The woman may prove to be just as vindictive as her son. You showing up there might only aggravate the situation and make matters worse," he cautioned.

Nikki stopped pacing to link her gaze with his. "I have to do something, Paul. I have to protect Amy...maybe... maybe if I go there and appeal to her motherly instincts, she'll understand tha—"

"Nikki, you're not a mother remember. You going there and doing that has the potential of having the exact opposite effect than what you intended," Paul spoke out in frustration.

Nikki froze at his words. *You're not a mother.*

"You couldn't give me what I needed more than anything, Nikki, so I had to get it from somewhere. What did you expect? I wanted children even before we got married. There is no way in hell I was gonna stick around knowing you can't give me the one thing I want more than anything. I tried. Believe me, I tried. But this isn't enough anymore. Roxanne is pregnant, and I need to be a father to my child and create a stable home environment for him. I can't do that and remain married to you. I want a divorce."

Those words and the betrayal had cut Nikki so deep that when her ex Josh left to be with his mistress he'd secretly been in a relationship with for over three years, she had suffered a total mental breakdown. If she hadn't had Ava and her go-to bottle of Pinot Noir to occasionally sip or chug, she was certain she would have been admitted to the asylum. She remembered how devastatingly inadequate she had felt knowing that the one thing Josh wanted and she wanted, her body wouldn't cooperate to produce.

Her heart tightened as the pain from all those years came crashing down on her, the weight squeezing her chest and threatening to crush her.

"Hey. You okay?" Paul asked, waving his hand before her face.

"Of course, I'm okay. Tell you what, the minute I'm not okay, you'll be the first to know," Nikki said with an attitude, her head shaking vigorously with each word.

Paul reared back in surprise, his eyes widening.

175

"What's wrong? Was it something I said?" Paul questioned with concern in his voice. His eyes widened, and his mouth opened wide as realization dawned on him.

"Nikki, I'm—I...I didn't mean...that didn't come out right." The words came tumbling out of his mouth as he tried to apologize.

"Can you go? I'm not feeling well." She turned her back to him.

"Nikki..."

"Please, Paul, just go," she said forcefully, keeping her eyes fixed on the wall. When he got up and headed for the door, she followed and slowly closed it on him as he stared at her regretfully. Nikki broke down immediately after, the crushing pain in her chest causing her to collapse and sag against the wall.

Chapter Twenty-Two

Paul sat in his office back at Lot 28 going over the numbers. So far, everything seemed to be on track for the establishment to have another successful year; guest numbers had greatly increased since the start of summer and kept trending high. He was satisfied.

He sighed for what felt like the umpteenth time, and he reclined in his chair twirling the pen around his fingers as his mood became pensive.

He'd hurt Nikki. Even though it had not been his intention, the hurt look on her face showed just how much his words had cut her deep. If he could have retracted his statement, he would have, then he wouldn't have to be in his office thinking about her, wondering if she was all right or what he could do to make it up to her. He hadn't exactly left her in the best of moods. She had been highly charged and refused to listen to anything else after he'd reminded her that she wasn't a mother. Seeing her so upset and knowing that he was the reason for it caused his heart to ache. He put his hand over his chest and massaged the area above the scar he'd received from the surgery.

Just then, there was a knock on the door before the head chef and his partner stepped into the office, and his hand fell away from his chest.

"You look like hell," Ken observed as he settled into the sofa at the far corner of the office, his perceptive eyes trained on Paul.

"I'm fine. I'm just a little fatigued after reviewing the books for the past two hours." He plastered a smile on his face that he hoped was convincing enough.

"You know you could have left. I could have finished it for you. Don't want you having another...episode if it can be prevented."

"What did you want to talk to me about?" Paul asked, changing the subject.

Ken didn't speak for a while but continued eyeing him as if trying to figure something out. Paul felt like squirming under the scrutiny.

"The business has been doing so well and the restaurant keeps having such a huge draw and great reviews, even the one back at the Nestled Inn...I was thinking that we could maybe branch out. What do you think about opening another Lot 28 in Seattle?"

Paul nodded his head contemplatively as he thought about his partner's suggestion. Another one Michelin star restaurant opening would be great for their brand. However...

"It's a good idea. I can see us drawing in an even greater crowd if we open a sister branch in Seattle..."

"But?" Ken asked, noting his hesitation.

"I'll have to talk to Sarah about it. After everything that's happened, she worries about me even more than I worry about myself, you know? And I tell her everything. If she's fine with it, then I'm definitely on board. But there's a lot to think about with starting this new venture too like the starting capital, recruiting only the best of the best to run the restaurant..."

"Let me worry about that part. Just talk to Sarah and see what she says," Ken assured him.

Paul nodded his agreement.

"So..."

"What?" Paul asked, noting the glint in his friend's eye and the smirk lifting the corners of his mouth.

"What's the deal between you and Nikki?"

"What do you mean?" Paul asked, furrowing his brows.

Ken leaned forward and placed his hands on his raised knees. "I mean, are you guys dating?"

"What? No. No, Nikki and I are just friends," Paul sputtered.

"You sure about that? I've seen the way you look at her, and that, my friend, is more than just friendly." Ken wagged his eyebrows suggestively.

"She. Is. Only. A. Friend," Paul stressed. But he didn't sound too convincing, even to his own ears. She was his friend that he liked a little more than just a friend. He couldn't deny that.

Back in high school, he'd seen a whole future with her. Then life happened. She left him and went off to college to become a big shot journalist. However, the attraction he'd felt for her all those years ago resurfaced the moment he saw her standing there in her sister's doorway, a surprised smile on her lips as her blue-gray eyes shined brightly at him. At that moment, he had been transported back to all his dreams for them, back when he thought they were meant to spend the rest of their lives together. No one told him that it rarely ever ended that way with your first love. Paul shook himself out of the memory.

Those were dangerous thoughts to entertain, especially now that he wasn't sure Nikki was what he wanted at this stage of his life or if he was even what she needed with everything she was battling. Maybe it was better that the past remained just that—the past.

A hand waved before his face, bringing him out of his reverie.

"I lost you a while back there," his friend said when he turned to focus on him.

"Sorry about that. Are we still on for that fishing trip up Puget Sound?" he asked, changing the subject again.

If Ken realized what he had done, he had made no attempt to call Paul out on it.

"Are you kidding me? I've been ready for this trip since we made the plans," he spoke happily. "There is no way I'm not gonna be on that boat come Saturday. I have everything set; even the hooks and rod are in my shed, and I'm picking the bait up Friday afternoon."

"Looks to me like you've been planning for this trip your whole life." Paul smirked.

"And then some," his friend replied solemnly as a faraway look came into his eyes.

Paul inclined his head in understanding. His friend had never been fishing before because between going to law school and jumping through hoops to please his parents, he simply hadn't had the time to experience the joys of things like fishing. The most gratifying thing he'd done for himself was to quit the law firm he worked at for nearly half his life to invest in and help Paul run Lot 28.

"Don't worry, friend. I'll make sure you have a memorable experience. We can make a tradition of it."

Ken smiled appreciatively.

As soon as his friend left the office to prepare for the afternoon lunch rush, Paul again turned his attention to the books. Only, he couldn't focus on what was in those books because he had just one thing on his mind, or rather one person. Nikki.

Thoughts of high school came flashing into his mind once more. He remembered how inseparable he and Nikki had been. He also remembered the devastation he had felt when she suggested they break up after prom because they were going to different colleges, charting different paths. He'd put up a brave front and agreed with her even though his heart had felt like someone was holding it tightly in their fist and squeezing the life out of it. The ring he'd saved up all of his allowances and money from working at the Shack to buy had weighed heavily in his pocket while he carried it around, preparing to propose to Nikki at their senior prom. But after the bombshell she'd dropped, it had felt like it was searing a hole in his pocket. He had stood there on the beach with her, listening to the waves crash against the rocky banks, the salt air swirling around them and causing Nikki's blond hair to levitate as it covered her face. He'd plastered a smile as he'd agreed with her assertions. Years after the breakup, he'd pined after her, but then he'd met Natalie.

At the thought of his late wife, guilt engulfed him. He knew, without a doubt, that he had loved her and had made the right choice to marry and start a family with her. He would not have changed anything about his life, but realizing that he had carried these feelings for Nikki all these years felt like a betrayal to what he'd shared with Natalie.

He remembered the first time he saw Natalie. They were taking the same elective course, Modern Philosophy. He remembered how she'd come bustling into the class halfway through.

"Therefore, Descartes is considered the founder of what we term modern philoso—"

A young woman came barreling into the room, cutting off the lecturer's words and directing all the eyes in the room to her rather noisy entrance.

"Care to explain why you came barging in in the middle of my lesson?" the lecturer asked, arms folded over his chest as he gave her a pointed look.

"I'm sorry, sir. I overslept, and then I couldn't find my notebook, and then my key got stuck in the keyhole of my dorm room—it nearly broke- and then my sho—"

"That's enough," the lecturer spoke, holding up a hand that effectively cut off whatever else the girl was about to say.

What caught Paul's attention was the shocking purple color at the end of her blond, curly hair and the eyebrow piercing that moved with every animated gesture when she spoke. He was intrigued, to say the least.

"See if you can find a seat and try not to interrupt the class anymore. Make sure you make it to your other classes on time."

The girl went to speak, but the lecturer held his hand up to halt her words. She turned and scanned the mostly packed room, trying to locate a seat when her eyes zeroed in on him or rather the seat that was right next to him. She gingerly picked her way through the rows and the sea of bodies whose eyes remained fixated on her, some of them holding condescending smirks. When she made it to the seat, she sat and stared ahead as the lecturer picked up where he'd left off.

"Hi."

Paul turned surprised eyes toward the girl who stared back at him with a broad, daring grin.

"Hi," he responded, carefully watching what the lecturer was doing from the corner of his eye.

"I know it's far out, but can I borrow your notes after class?" she asked.

"Um, sure," he replied.

"Great," the girl responded, pleased, before turning her head to the front of the class to listen to the lecturer. Paul did the same.

After the lecture, Paul stayed back, allowing her to copy his notes, and from that day onward, they had been inseparable.

He had been happy with Natalie. They'd had a wonderful life. She taught him how to be a good husband and a good father. There was, without a doubt, nothing he would change about their life together.

Still...

His thoughts kept going back to Nikki. To deny that Nikki was also in his heart would be to deny that what he had felt for her was akin to what you would call having a soulmate. But...

It still felt like a betrayal to Natalie's memory, and he did not know what to do about the dilemma he now found himself in.

Chapter Twenty-Three

Two days later

"Are ya ready, mate?"

Paul stared unblinking and horrified at the man standing before him in bright yellow fishing overalls, matching water boots, and a fishing hat with rubber hooks and fish adorning it.

"What in heavens are you wearing?" he asked in alarm.

"Whaddya mean?" Ken asked, looking over his ensemble.

"You remind me of a certain entertainer that usually wears that same color, but they also wear a lot of face makeup, a red nose, and a multicolored Afro," Paul responded.

"Ha ha, very funny," Ken deadpanned.

"Got any knock-knock jokes?" Paul asked, quaking with laughter.

"Tell you what, why don't I use your head as a door?

I'll knock, and you can tell me if it's funny." Ken advanced toward his friend with a determined glare.

"All right. I'm sorry," Paul called out, his hands raised in surrender. Ken stopped his advance.

"I won't call you a clown even though you're kinda dressed like one in that." Paul smirked triumphantly before turning around to head inside.

Something tapped against his temple, causing Paul to look over his shoulder. He saw Ken holding the object that had struck him.

"I hate to break it to you, friend, but we're not at Puget yet, so until then...no fishing," he said, moving the end of the fishing hook away from his face. Ken's face lit with a mischievous grin as he followed Paul inside.

"I just need to grab my gear, then we can head out," Paul called over his shoulder before disappearing through the door leading to the basement and leaving Ken in the foyer.

When he made his way back up, he found his friend in the living room, standing by the mantel and staring up at the portrait above it. It was one of him, Sarah, Natalie, and their Labrador Retriever, Skipper. They were huddled together with bright smiles and merry eyes staring at the camera while Skipper's tongue hung from his partially opened mouth.

Paul remembered the day the photo had been taken. They'd gone to the park for a family picnic. They'd had so much fun being together, bonding that Natalie felt the day couldn't end without them getting a family photo. The sides of his mouth quirked upward in a smile as his eyes glazed over at the memory. That had been the month before she found out about the leukemia, but by then, it had been too late. His lips slowly collapsed, and the smile disappeared.

"Ready to go?" he asked, bringing Ken's attention to his presence.

"Yeah. I'm ready," he turned to say with a simple smile.

When Ken brushed past him and headed for the foyer, Paul looked back at the smiling face of his late wife before turning and heading for the door with his friend. After attaching the small craft to the back of the car, they settled into their seats.

"I picked this up for you," Paul said, handing Ken the small square paper that was his permit to fish recreationally in the Washington State area.

"Thanks, man," Ken responded, inspecting the card.

With that, they were off to do some fishing. After driving down Camano Drive for three miles, Paul turned north, and after another three minutes, he parked to the left of the mounted historical sign at Utsalady Point. He and Ken unhooked the motorized rowboat and carried it down the path toward the boat launch.

"Man, I'll never get tired of a view like this," Ken said, with his hands folded across his chest staring out at the open water.

Paul followed his gaze and took in the breathtaking panorama that included the Cascade Mountains, Whidbey Island, and Skagit Bay in the distance. A smile graced his lips and he nodded in agreement with his friend and partner. "You definitely can't appreciate something like this living in the city," he added.

"Yeah," Ken returned.

"We can fish out in the open water, or maybe we can go to a great spot I know," Paul suggested as the two got into the boat, and he began to row away from the dock into the blue-green waters. A few boats were already out on the water as people took advantage of the great weather. A few larger sailboats could also be seen out on the horizon.

"Open-water fishing sounds fun." Ken made his choice.

"All right, open fishing it is, then," Paul agreed, taking the boat farther out toward the brackish water of the estuary. Killing the motor, he turned to Ken. "Okay, so just a few tips. When you've baited your hook, you'll throw the line out as far away from the boat as you can. As soon as you feel the line jerk and the bobber sinks, point your rod tip this way and pull back with a little pressure. When the lure is firmly settled in the fish's mouth, it'll start struggling to break free, but don't reel it in just yet. Give it time to tire out, then reel it in," he instructed.

"Aye aye, captain." Ken saluted with a smirk. He did exactly as Paul instructed, baiting the hook and throwing out his line.

Paul did the same, and the two sat in silence, as if afraid that any sound or sudden movement would scare their prey while they waited for them to take the bait.

Paul felt the boat jostle with the sudden movement from beside him. He looked over at Ken, his brows raised in question.

"I got something," Ken said excitedly.

"All right, remember what I told you?" Paul asked, scooting closer to him to monitor his progress. Ken nodded. Paul watched as the fishing rod slightly bent as whatever was at the end of the line struggled to break free.

"Lengthen the line. Reel it in but not too close," Paul

guided as Ken leaned forward, the spinning reel tightly clasped in his hand. He continued to do this for a good two minutes.

"Okay, looks like he's given up. Take your time and reel him in."

Ken took his time and reeled in his line until the silvery, scaly body of a sea bass broke the surface.

"Look at this beauty," he marveled when he finally got the fish into the boat. It was at least two feet in length and bulky in width.

"That is a beauty," Paul agreed with a nod as he looked from the triumphant grin on his friend's face to his catch. "Great job, Ken," he congratulated.

With his free hand, Ken pumped his fist in victory.

For the next couple of hours, the two men continued to throw out their lines, but Ken who was the amateur seemed to be having more luck in reeling in a number of big fishes while Paul sat caught in his own thoughts.

"Penny for your thoughts?"

"Hmm? What was that?" he asked, looking away from staring unseeingly into the clear water to Ken.

"I asked what was on your mind?" Ken responded. "Wait, don't tell me," he said with a bright, knowing smile. "I'm guessing it's on account of a woman? A certain blond with blue-gray eyes, to be exact," he said with a raised eyebrow and a smirk.

Paul gave his friend a tight-lipped smile before releasing a heavy sigh and turning to stare at the ripples fanning out across the water as the boat rocked from the slight gust. He was thinking about Nikki. The fact that he hadn't really talked to her in the past two days, besides a "hello," and a few questions about the restaurant and the B & B was driving him crazy. He'd wanted to apologize for how insensitive his comment had come off the other day, but he'd also been afraid that he would end up saying the wrong thing again and make the situation worse. He'd opted to stay quiet, mimicking Nikki, but their interactions were awkward at best with fleeting glances that said more than they were willing to share with each other. Plus, he needed to get his feelings in check. A slipup and him telling her exactly how he felt about her wasn't wise at this time. He didn't want to scare her away.

After what felt like a long time, Paul rolled his shoulders back to loosen the tension that tightened the muscles. "I have feelings for Nikki," he finally confessed to his friend in a low, somber tone.

When Ken didn't immediately respond, he glanced over at his friend with raised brows.

"I called it," Ken finally said, turning to him with a winning grin. "Want to talk about it?" he asked when Paul remained silent.

"We were high school sweethearts, but then she left to go to college to become a journalist, and I got over it. First love, you know? The only thing is it seems those feelings never left, and now that she's back and we've been spending time together...I can't help but wonder what it would have been like if she had stayed, what it would feel like now...I want to tell her how I feel." His shoulders relaxed after he shared his news with Ken. It felt like some load had been taken off them.

"I could have told you that a million times back," Ken joked. "The fact that you've been so distracted this whole trip... I reeled in more and the biggest fish in the river..." He pointed at the pile of fish on his side compared to Paul's own meager catch, then continued to talk. "If nothing else, it tells me that your feelings for her are pretty strong," he finished, agreeing with his own statement.

"Yeah," Paul replied, his mouth set in a grim line.

"Something tells me you're not pleased by that revelation," Ken predicted.

"Geez. What gave it away?" Paul's tone dripped with sarcasm.

Ken waited for his explanation.

Paul breathed in deeply before expelling the heavy, toxic air from his lungs. It did nothing to release the tight coils like binding wires swirling around in his stomach.

"I feel like I'm betraying Nat's memories...the life we built, shared together." He looked over at his friend briefly, his face painted with the guilt he felt before turning back to the water.

"I may not be able to tell you exactly what you need to hear, but I believe Nat would want you to be happy, Paul. It's okay to love more than one person, especially when they come into your life at the right time. The time they are needed the most." Ken reached over to rest a hand on Paul's shoulder, prompting him to turn and look at him. "Nat would want you to be happy," Ken spoke earnestly.

Paul gave his friend a lopsided smile as he considered all that he'd said. He could already see himself having a future. Although it scared him—a lot—maybe it was time he started accepting those visions; enough to start making them a reality. If his relationship with Nikki had the potential to head in that direction, he didn't want to make the same mistakes as before.

"All right, enough about my love life or lack thereof. Let's get back to fishing. I have a lot of making up to do. I'm going to show you what a pro fisherman can do," he said, giving Ken a smile of challenge.

"Bring it on, but be prepared to lose to me because I'm a natural at this," Ken countered with an equally daring grin.

The two men didn't leave Puget Sound until the sky flashed orange and pink over the horizon as the sun retreated.

After dropping Ken off at home, Paul took a detour from going home and found himself on Trish's front porch. He rang the doorbell.

Nikki answered on the third ring, and Paul's heart beat wildly in his chest at the sight of her standing in the doorway, staring back at him in surprise and hesitancy.

"Hi. I went fishing, and I thought you might want some." He spoke in a nervous rush as his heart continued to accelerate almost to the point of beating out of his chest. He held up the bag of fish for her to see.

"Thank you," Nikki replied softly as she held the door. "I really appreciate it," she continued, reaching for the bag and gesturing with her chin for him to follow her inside. He walked with her toward the kitchen and stood by the island as he watched her transfer the fish to a ziplock bag. After putting them in the freezer, she finally turned to face him, her eyes steeped with caution.

Paul opened his mouth to speak, but nothing came out. His mind felt like it was in a time warp, and his thoughts were all over the place, making it difficult to form a coherent sentence.

"Paul?" Nikki stared at him in confusion and concern. "What's wro—"

"I'm sorry!" he blurted, startling her. Nikki's brows furrowed, and her arms came up to rest across her chest.

Paul cleared his throat before continuing. "I'm sorry about what I said the other day. I wasn't thinking, but I wasn't trying to hurt you, I promise. The truth is I lo..."

Nikki's arms slowly fell to her sides, and her eyes widened as her lips parted.

"I-I, um..." Paul averted his eyes as his hand reached up to scratch the back of his neck nervously while he tried to collect his thoughts. "I love our friendship, Nikki, and I can't imagine losing it...losing you," he said, his gaze once more on her. "The last couple of days have been torment-ing. I really do wish I could take back what I said."

"Friends," Nikki said softly, looking down at the floor as frown lines creased the corners of her mouth. "Okay, friends, it is...that's what we are, friends, and I forgive you Paul," she said, her eyes leveling with his once more and a thin smile on her lips.

Paul released a relieved breath, but his chest still felt queasy as he stared at her. He couldn't shake the feeling that he had said the wrong thing—again.

Chapter Twenty-Four

"Where do these go?" Nikki held up the stack of towels she'd just removed from the basket she'd brought upstairs to one of the guest rooms she was helping to prep for the arrival of new guests.

"They go on the second shelf to your left," Kaylin responded, pointing at the custom built-in closet that took up at least half of the back wall in the room.

Complying, Nikki carefully organized the towels on the shelves before moving to put a pair of bathrobes on the shelf below it.

"Should I change the curtains?" she turned to ask the woman now, smoothing out the wrinkles from the cotton sheets she'd spread over the queen-sized pillowtop mattress and fluffing the feathered pillows.

"Oh no, Dorothy changed those only a day ago. What you can do, though, is open the windows and let in some of that fresh air," Kaylyn advised.

Nikki walked across the multicolored woolen carpet covering most of the floor not housing a piece of furniture.

Pushing aside the light beige curtains, she threw open the French windows with a welcomed sigh as the cool breeze burst into the room, bringing with it the slight saltiness of the sea.

"Thank you for agreeing to help me get these rooms ready, Nikki. With Dorothy being sick and all, I appreciate the help," Kaylyn spoke with a smile of gratitude.

"I'm happy I could help. How is Dorothy by the way?" Nikki asked.

"She sounded a lot better than she did yesterday, but I told her not to come in until she is a hundred percent better," Kaylyn replied.

"That's wise," Nikki agreed, returning to the basket to organize the rest of the linen in their respective places.

When she was finished, she stepped back to look at her handiwork before turning to take a better look at the room. She liked the light flowery patterns on the walls and the light furnishings, accentuated by the row of cushion in the little nook at the far corner that gave the room a more endearing and homey feel to it. Overall, she approved of the decor that was duplicated in most of the rooms.

"You know, when Trish bought this place, it was a little more than just a condemned building. It had a sturdy framework, but inside was a total disaster. You can say she had to start from scratch to get this place to where it is now," Kaylyn informed her, her voice taking on a tone of respect and admiration as she talked about Trish.

Nikki approached the woman, her head bobbing slowly to indicate her interest in the rest of the story.

Kaylyn didn't need any more invitation than that. "She had to take out all of the carpets and get the floor surfaced with hardwood. A majority of the kitchen came from IKEA. The upstairs was just one big space, but when Trish finished, it ended up being three bedrooms in addition to the three on the ground floor."

"She did a really good job," Nikki marveled, looking around the room again.

Kaylyn turned to look at Nikki, her eyes softening as she continued to speak. "Your sister sacrificed so much to make this place what it is because she wanted you to be proud of her and what she was able to accomplish. She wanted you to know and for you to see that she had taken charge of her life."

Nikki's eyes widened in surprise at the news. "I didn't know she felt that way...that I wasn't proud of her...she never said anything," she responded softly, her voice filled with sadness and remorse.

Kaylyn reached out to rest a warm, comforting hand against her arm as she gave her a knowing smile. "She tried to reach out to you on a number of occasions but each time she would get cold feet. She's never stopped loving and respecting you, Nikki. She was...she is proud that you are her sister, and your opinion matters to her a great deal," the woman finished, her words echoing in Nikki's ears with the potency of their impact.

She gave the woman a smile of gratitude. "Thanks for letting me know."

Kaylyn returned her smile before letting her hand drop from her arm and getting the toiletries they'd brought up to place in the bathrooms. The two worked like that for the next half hour, freshening the unoccupied rooms as they continued with small talk.

Nikki left Kaylyn upstairs to go man the receptionist's desk when Amy came barreling through the door. A smile that ran from ear to ear brightened her face as her eyes shone with delight.

"Someone's happy," Nikki surmised with a smile of her own as she stared back at her niece.

Amy held up a manila envelope in response.

"Is that what I think it is?" Nikki asked, her excitement level going up.

Amy's head nodded vigorously. "I got into culinary school," she beamed, waving the letter proudly.

"Oh my! That's great. I knew you could do it," Nikki replied, reaching for her niece and bringing her in for a tight hug. "Where?" she asked when they separated.

"Here, The Camano Island School of Culinary Arts," Amy answered.

"Even better," Nikki responded joyfully.

"Classes start in the fall so I have a little time to get my tools together," Amy informed her.

"That's good. In the meantime, you can continue going to Lot 28 to hone your skills, maybe pick up a few more hours if you're up to it," Nikki suggested.

"That's what Paul said back at the restaurant."

Amy's response caught Nikki by surprise. "You saw Paul?"

"Yeah, he was there today going over the menu with the head chef, and then he had lunch with Aaron," Amy explained.

"Sarah's fiancé?" she asked.

Amy nodded.

"Okay...and you told him about your acceptance letter?"

"Yeah, I told him. Is that a problem?" Amy asked, her brows furrowed in concern.

"No. No. That's okay. I'm really glad he's in your

corner," Nikki replied with a smile that didn't quite reach her eyes.

She didn't know why she felt so put out by her niece sharing the news with Paul before her, but it felt different from the way she'd felt all the other times when it felt like Amy related more to him than she did to her. Her thoughts flashed to his apology a few days ago and him expressing that he cherished her as a friend. Again, she couldn't quite figure out why she had been disappointed by his declaration. She didn't even want to examine it, fearing she wouldn't like the answer.

"Amy, sweetheart, how are you?" Kaylyn, who'd just walked down the stairs, greeted the young woman.

"I got into culinary school," Amy informed her, waving the envelope.

"Oh, that's wonderful," Kaylyn expressed, bringing Amy into a tight hug as she congratulated her.

"Let me get in on this action," Nikki said, opening her arms wide enough to cover the two women in her own embrace. They all bubbled with laughter and joy at the great news.

The day before the fundraising

"Could you check on the cupcakes, please?" Amy called out to her aunt as she flitted around the kitchen. They were baking in preparation for the fundraiser.

Nikki walked over to the oven and gingerly lowered the door to check on the cupcakes like Amy asked. "They look okay. They'll definitely be ready the second the timer goes off," she informed her niece as she straightened up. The whole kitchen had been transformed into a bakery. There wasn't a surface that didn't have trays of cookies, brownies, cupcakes, and pies. The sweet smell of the freshly baked confections filled the whole house with their savory scent.

"Great," Amy replied, relaxing as she creamed the sugar and butter to make the icing she would use to decorate the cupcakes.

Nikki smiled as she watched her niece. She would make an excellent pastry chef. "I'm going by the restaurant to see how they're doing."

"Okay," Amy replied.

Nikki walked out of the kitchen and headed for the front door. She breathed out a sigh of satisfaction when the cool night air washed over her warm skin. It had been exceptionally hot working in the kitchen with Amy but very much worth it. Amy was in her element, doing what she loved, and Nikki was proud of her. It was just a pity she had to go through all the trauma she had to arrive at this moment. Brushing the troublesome thought away, she made her way down the porch steps and walked along the walkway lit by the diffused light from the solar lamps lining both sides. She went past the inn and then turned at the wooden arrow pointing at the restaurant. She pushed the glass door open to enter the restaurant. It had been closed early so that the workers who'd volunteered to stay back and help prepare the food for the event the next day had enough time to do so.

"Good evening, ladies," Nikki greeted the two wait-staff in the main dining area, removing the tablecloths from the tables and wiping them down.

"Good evening, Miss Nikki," they greeted back with smiles of their own. "Chef Ryan and the others are in the kitchen," one of them informed her.

"Thank you, and keep up the good work," she threw

back at them as she headed for the kitchen. The women beamed with pride.

Like back at the house, there was a flurry of activities —the chef and his team mixing, chopping, stirring, and tasting the food they were preparing.

Upon seeing her, Chef Ryan, who'd been talking to one of the cooks, came walking over to her and smiled.

"Everything looks and smells great," Nikki said in greeting. "Thank you so much for doing this, Ryan. I appreciate it, and I know Trish will appreciate it too," she spoke in a hopeful tone.

"Are you kidding me? We're all happy to do this. We've all been wondering what we can do to help. We love Trish. She's family to all of us. Plus, this fundraiser is a great way to honor her, and we're all on board with it," Ryan said with a reassuring smile.

Nikki smiled gratefully. Trish really had a dream team to work with. The way they all loved and respected her spoke to the good heart she knew Trish had all along. After going over the menu for the event, Nikki took her leave and headed for the main house.

Just as she opened the front door and was about to step inside, the headlights of a car easing into the driveway caught her attention. She recognized that it was Paul's car, and her heartbeat multiplied. He stepped out of the vehicle wearing a V-neck T-shirt and cargo shorts and looking unnaturally handsome with his tousled dark brown hair and a few strands falling over his forehead. Her heart rate skyrocketed.

Nikki couldn't fight the bright smile that took over her face or the knowledge that her cheeks were probably flushed as she watched him ascend the two steps leading up the porch. The butterflies in her stomach wreaked havoc. Familiar emotions stirred within her as the faintest spent of his aftershave infiltrated her nostrils. In that instant with his smiling face inching closer to her, Nikki was finally able to admit she had feelings for Paul Thompson; feelings that probably never left her all these years.

Chapter Twenty-Five

"Hello dear, you don't know me, but I know your sister. She was a real gem. As busy as she was with running her business and serving on the committee of the Humane Society, she still found time to spend with little old me...I sure do miss her, as do our bridge club."

"Thank you, Miss...?"

"Just call me Etta, dear," the woman replied with a broad grin on her wrinkled face.

Nikki nodded with a smile. "Etta, thank you for your kind words. I'm sure Trish will let you know just how appreciative she is of your praises when she wakes up."

A look of doubt flashed in the woman's eyes before her lips turned up in a smile, and her head rocked back and forth. "I will continue to pray for a miracle," the woman said, placing a feeble hand on Nikki's upper arm.

Nikki returned the smile, though not as enthusiastically as she had at the beginning of the conversation. When the old woman walked off, she puffed out a breath of annoyance. She knew the people meant well, and she didn't doubt their sincere shows of affection for her sister, but it was also evident that a few of the folks had given up on her regaining consciousness, and that annoyed her because there was a niggling doubt at the back of her mind that it was a possibility.

Collecting her thoughts, she schooled her expression and fixed a smile on her lips as she turned back to the people and the festivities. Lot 28 had been transformed into an open space decorated with balloons and streamers. Potted bamboo palms and succulents lined the room's sides and corners, and an orchid stood regally before the podium. The banner that flew above the podium was thoughtful in its representation of Trish while inspiring hope—The Trisha Murphy Foundation (Raising Funds For Those Who Can't Do It For Themselves). She liked it very much.

"Your sister sure will make a fuss when she wakes up and realizes she has a fund named in her honor. Serves her well too. She's given enough to be rewarded for it, whether she likes it or not."

"Hi, Nelly." Nikki turned and smiled at the woman beside her, looking up at the banner. "I haven't been here long, but I agree with you 100 percent. Trish deserves this honor and so much more." She turned to stare up at the banner again. "I just wish she was awake to witness it all." She bowed her head, and her eyes fluttered shut, her emotions threatening to overtake her.

Nikki felt the small, fragile grip of Nelly's fingers around her upper arm. She opened her eyes to stare into the determined gray eyes of the older woman.

"Trish will be fine. That one, she's a fighter," Nelly spoke confidently before allowing her hand to fall away from Nikki's arm.

A small, grateful smile lifted the corners of Nikki's mouth as hope blossomed in her chest once more. She knew in her heart of hearts, then, that Trish would be okay.

"Let's get you a chair so you can rest," Nikki suggested, hooking the old woman's hand with hers.

"I know you probably can't eat anything here, but would you like some punch? It's natural," she offered Nelly after settling her on a cushioned seat.

"Got any lemonade?" Nelly asked, smiling up at Nikki.

"I'll check." With that, Nikki walked toward the serving area. Ryan and his team and a few volunteers recruited by Reed were in charge of monitoring and sharing the food. Nikki marveled at how many choices were available to the people.

Before she could make it to the table displaying the beverages, a couple walked in her path, stopping her in her tracks.

"Hi, my name is Sally, and this is my husband, Karl Shetty," the woman said with a bright smile on her lips.

"Nice to meet you." Nikki smiled, reaching for the hand the lady stretched to her before doing the same with her husband.

"How did you know Trish?" she asked them.

"I met her a year ago. I came to volunteer at the Humane Society, and she was there. She was very friendly and helpful. It's because of her that we even have a cat."

"That sounds like Trish." Nikki smiled in encouragement.

"She was also instrumental in my meeting Karl because she encouraged me to follow my heart and give him a chance. I did, and look at us now." The woman smiled lovingly up at the man with his hand around her, already smiling affectionately back at her.

"Trish is a phenomenal woman," a proud Nikki responded with a wide grin. It was beginning to look like a recurring theme that her sister had left the lives of those she interacted with transformed in some way or another.

Finally excusing herself, she made it to the drinks section and got Nelly a cup of lemonade and a fruit punch for herself.

"Here you go, Nelly," she said, handing the woman the cold beverage.

"Thank you, dear," she responded, taking the glass and bringing it to her lips almost immediately. "Where's that lovely niece of yours?" she asked Nikki after a few sips.

"She's at the house with Paul. They're packaging the pastries to bring here for the guests," she informed the old woman whose head bobbed in understanding. "We've got quite the turnout," she mused, looking around the almost packed room. Paul had mentioned that about forty people could hold in the space comfortably, but at least double that number of persons were on the outside patio and surrounding lawn sipping wine, chatting, and laughing. The soft jazz music floating out in the air created a laid-back atmosphere.

"Your sister is well-loved by the residents of Camano Island. The minute persons became aware of this event, they were ready to throw in their support," Nelly informed her.

"I'm blown away every time someone speaks about her," Nikki confessed. She noticed Reed motioning to her from across the room. "Excuse me for a minute Nelly."

With that, she walked over to the man whose demeanor told her something wasn't right.

"Hey, Reed. What's wrong?" she asked in concern.

"I think I underprojected. More people are arriving for the fundraiser by the minute, and I'm afraid there won't be enough food to feed them all." He scratched the back of his head nervously as his eyes darted outside to the patio before focusing on her once more. "I don't want to let everyone down...this event was supposed to be perfect. Trish deserves only the best," he rambled on, his voice a mix of frustration and disappointment.

Nikki placed a hand on his shoulder in calming reassurance. "Reed, listen to me, relax. You did a fantastic job. No one will fault you for doing your best. Trish would be overwhelmed with gratitude if she was here right now," she spoke convincingly. "Besides, Paul has Lot 28 on standby to make up for any food shortage we may have if the crowd gets too overwhelming."

Reed's shoulders relaxed, and he breathed out in relief. A smile appeared on his lips. "Thanks, Nikki, I think I needed that. I just want everything to be perfect for Trish...I mean for the foundation we're setting up in her name."

Nikki smiled knowingly but said nothing about his earlier statement.

"I'll be sure to thank Paul for all the help he's been giving," Reed finished, and Nikki nodded in agreement.

"I have a suggestion," she said, looking over at the man staring back at her with interest.

"What's that?" he asked.

"For the speech you're going to give, why don't we move it to the outside? We can take the podium out there, and that way, everyone will be able to participate better."

"That's a good idea," he agreed. "I'll get someone to help me take it outside."

Reed moved off to find someone to help him with the task, and Nikki smiled in glee at his retreating back. If she weren't already sure, Reed's mini-freak-out and his slipup about the foundation was enough for her to know that the man's feelings for her sister ran very deep. She couldn't wait to witness their awkward phase of tiptoeing around each other instead of admitting how they really felt. Kind of like what she and Paul were doing. She smiled wryly.

Nikki spent a couple more minutes greeting the people who had known Trish and had so many stories to tell about how they knew her. With each passing comment, her love and respect for Trish grew even more.

Paul and Amy brought over the thank-you boxes filled with treats for their guests before joining her outside as they prepared for Reed to give his speech about the fundraiser.

Nikki stood looking behind the podium at the vast ocean in the distance. The waves crashed over each other in white foamy splendor as they raced for the sandy shores. She felt the presence of someone beside her, and she looked over to see her niece, who turned to smile at her. She felt another presence on her opposite side, and she looked over to see Paul standing there. Although the time was relatively warm, even with the breeze coming in from the ocean, Nikki felt the fine ridges of goose bumps raise along her bare arms as the butterflies rushed in to take a comfortable seat in her chest. Paul looked over and smiled. Her lips automatically raised at the corners in response. Just then, Reed began to talk, and Nikki turned to focus on what he was saying.

"As you all are aware, our beloved Trish was in an

accident some time ago and has been in a coma ever since. We are still confident she will wake up soon because she is a fighter."

There were murmurs of agreement to Reed's latter statement, bringing a smile to Nikki's lips.

"Trish was and still is a force to be reckoned with. She cares deeply for the things she's involved in, and more importantly, she has a deep love for this community. It is why she joined the Humane Society and dedicated her time and resources to rehabilitating the many stray animals we've housed over the years while working to find suitable homes for them. Trish believed that if an animal's spirit that has been broken can be restored, then so can that of humans. She always tried to find families who needed to be reminded that there was meaning in their lives and that to love is truly a gift to be cherished."

A tear ran down Nikki's cheek as she listened to Reed's speech. Her sister was a true saint. She just wished she would wake up so she could tell her how much she loved her and was proud of her.

"While Trish is regaining her strength, her sister, Nikki, has been here working upfront and behind the scenes, maintaining Trish's legacy, and today, we want to applaud her for that."

All eyes turned to her as applause rang all around her. Nikki smiled sheepishly. When the clapping died down, Reed continued.

"We hope you will continue to serve on the board, Nikki. You have been doing a great job, and we are happy to have you."

Amy reached over to intertwine their fingers, and Nikki smiled before bumping her shoulder with hers affectionately.

She felt another pair of eyes on her, and she turned to see Paul staring back at her with admiration.

He leaned forward and whispered against her ear. "In case you didn't already know, you are a phenomenal woman too, Nikki."

She ducked her head as her cheeks heated, and an ear-splitting grin appeared on her lips. She looked back at him when she was sure she'd gotten her blushing under control.

"Thank you for everything, Paul. I don't think I could have gotten through this without your help." She smiled appreciatively at him.

"I'm happy I could," he responded, his eyes shining with emotion as he stared at her.

Nikki felt her heartbeat quicken, and she turned to listen to the rest of what Reed was saying.

She felt a tug on her fingers and looked over at her niece, who raised her brow suggestively.

Nikki rolled her eyes at her playfully. Just then, she felt her phone vibrate against her leg, and she reached into her pocket to retrieve it. Her brows furrowed, and her heart froze mid-thump at the number calling. Slowly, she brought it to her ear.

"Hello?" she answered. "Yes, this is Nikki," she replied, listening attentively to what the person on the other end of the line was saying.

Paul and Amy stared in concern at her.

When she finally ended the call, she turned to them.

"That was the hospital...Trish is awake."

Chapter Twenty-Six

Amy held on tightly to Nikki's hand as they settled in the back seat of Paul's car while he and Reed rode up front. The closer they got to the hospital, the louder Nikki's heart pounded against her chest. She was about to see her sister alive and awake after coming so close to losing her. She could feel the angst emanating from her niece, who stared out the window of the moving car while keeping a tight grip on her hand. Nikki looked down and noticed that her knuckles were drained of color. She wished she knew what she was thinking.

When she'd broken the news to Reed, and he had shared it with the guests, there had been loud cheers of joy. The relief on some of the faces was palpable. Reed had left his right hand in charge of the rest of the afternoon as he opted to go with them to the hospital. A couple more cars were traveling behind them with some close friends and well-wishers. Amy had frozen in place when she first broke the news, and after that, she seemed to be on autopilot. She hadn't said one word since entering the car. Nikki stared worriedly at her for a few seconds. Just then, the hospital came into view.

Nikki wasn't sure what she was expecting to see when she finally made it into the room, but in the meantime, her anxiety seemed to be getting the better of her.

"You guys okay?" Paul turned to ask them after he'd parked the car.

"I don't know," Amy answered truthfully, releasing a heavy sigh.

Nikki looked over at her to see the uncertainty flickering in her eyes. Tamping down her own insecurities, Nikki squeezed the hand she still held in hers and used her other hand to run soothingly down Amy's arm.

Amy turned to her, looking lost and afraid.

"Everything will be okay," she said with a reassuring smile. Opening the car door, she pulled Amy along until they stood face-to-face on the pavement. Nikki reached over and pulled her niece into her arms.

"I'm scared," Amy whispered to her.

"I know, sweetie, I know," Nikki replied, smoothing the hair at her temples lovingly. "Everything will be fine," she repeated, taking Amy's cheeks into her palms so she could stare into her eyes. "I promise."

Amy finally nodded, and the two women turned to the men waiting for them. After pushing through the lobby's entrance, they made their way to the elevator to take them up to Trish's wing.

Nikki's feet felt like someone had thrown cement in her shoes. The others followed closely when she made it off the elevator and walked over to the nurses' station.

"Hi, I'm here to see Trisha Murphy. They called to say she's awake," she managed to say.

"And you are?" the woman asked, looking through the

files on her desk. Nikki had never seen this woman before when she visited Trish, which would explain why she didn't know her.

"My name is Nikki Murphy. I'm her sister."

"Okay. Just a moment, let me get the doctor for you." The nurse reached for the telephone and spoke into the receiver before hanging up and turning to Nikki. "He'll be here in a few minutes. In the meantime, you and the others may have a seat," the woman informed her. Nikki couldn't sit. Instead, she paced the waiting area impatiently.

"Dad?"

Nikki looked up to see Sarah, Paul's daughter, walk toward him.

"Hey, sweetheart," Paul greeted her with a hug and a kiss against her temple.

"I was making my rounds when one of the nurses told me they saw you come up here. Is everything okay?" Sarah asked when they separated.

"It's Trish. They said she's awake," Paul replied.

"Oh, that's great news," Sarah responded.

"We haven't been in to see her yet, though. We're waiting on the doctor."

Sarah nodded in understanding before inclining her head to look behind him. Paul looked behind him too before turning back to her with a subtle nod.

Nikki watched Sarah walk over to her niece, who could only be described as shivering as she held herself against the wall.

"Hey, Amy," Sarah spoke softly as she came to stand before her.

Amy gave her a weak smile, a myriad of emotions swimming in her eyes.

"Oh, come here." Sarah drew her into her arms, and after a few tense seconds, Amy's arms came up to hug her back.

Nikki felt warmed by their interaction, and a smile made its way to her face as the scene before her chased away the nerves dancing to a strange beat in her stomach. Her eyes sought out Paul. He was already staring back at her with a knowing glint. His head inclined, acknowledging some unspoken confirmation about the two young women. Just then, Trish's doctor walked in.

"Ms. Murphy, how are you?" he greeted Nikki as he came to a stop before her with a bright smile.

"Honestly? I'm nervous," she confessed, clasping her hands before her.

"That's to be expected, but you needn't worry. Trish's vitals have improved a great deal since she woke up. She is conscious of who she is, so that's a good sign that there is little to no permanent neural disruptions. I must caution you however that she is still a bit out of it, so don't mention anything about the accident because we don't want to overwhelm her. That could delay her progress significantly."

"Thank you so much, Dr. Smith," Nikki replied, grateful for his explanation of her sister's current state. "Can I see her now?"

"Yes, of course, but only one or two at a time," the man advised her.

Nikki turned to Amy and held out her hand for her to take it. Amy's eyes widened in surprise, and her mouth opened and closed as she tried to speak, but in the end, she jerked her head from side to side.

Nikki walked over to her niece and gently entwined

their fingers. "You don't have to be afraid, Amy. I'm sure you are the first person Trish would want to see."

Amy's chest rose and fell rapidly as her eyes shuttered. She swallowed, slackening the tension in her jaw as her eyes slowly opened. Her head hesitantly nodded, and that was all the agreement Nikki needed. She gently pulled her niece toward the room Trish was in.

After a slight pause, Nikki pushed the door open and entered the room. The beep of the machines and the tubes running from Trish's arms and her nose were there like before, but as Nikki slowly approached the bed, she noted that her sister no longer wore an oxygen mask, and the ventilator was pushed to one side of the room. Trish's chest rose and fell freely, and this brought a relieved smile to Nikki's lips. Her hands went up to cover her mouth, and she looked down at her sister before turning to look at Amy, who remained by the door. Nikki turned back to Trish and took the remaining steps until she stood above her.

Nikki reached down and took her sister's hand in hers and leaned forward until she was a few inches from her face. "Trish, it's me, Nikki," she whispered softly.

Trish's eyes flew open almost instantly, and tears pooled in their depths when they finally focused on Nikki, who had tears of joy and relief flowing down her cheeks as well.

"Nikki," Trish spoke, her voice coming out weak and brittle as she continued to stare up at her as if unable to believe her eyes.

"Hey, Sis." Nikki gave her a watery smile.

"Nikki," Trish repeated, a smile finally turning up the corners of her mouth. She tried to raise her arms but could only move them a few inches above the bed.

Nikki gathered her in her arms, holding her carefully so as not to disturb the needles in her arms. Tears flowed freely down her face as she sobbed with both joy and remorse. "Oh my God, Trish, I thought I lost you," she wept. "I don't know what I would have done if I lost you."

Trish managed to raise one of her hands, and she patted Nikki's head reassuringly. "I'm here," she forced out.

After a good minute, Nikki disentangled herself from her sister and sat in the chair before bed. She reached out to lovingly run her palm down Trish's cheek. "I'm really sorry we grew apart. All those years...I should have done something, more than I did..." Noticing the look of distress on her sister's face, she quickly changed the subject. "We can talk about all that another time when you're much stronger. There's someone here you've been dying to meet." She smiled brightly.

As if suddenly realizing they weren't alone, Trish's eyes darted toward the door where Amy stood looking over at her with already wet eyes. Trish's hand went to her mouth as she stared in shock at her daughter. More tears flowed down her cheeks, a guttural sound forcing its way through her lips. She lifted her hand as far as she could, beckoning for Amy to come closer.

Slowly, Amy walked over to the bed and grasped the hand her mother held out to her. Nikki slid out of the chair and walked to one corner of the room with a smile on her lips.

"A-A-Amy?" Trish asked, even as the tears blurred her vision.

"Yeah...it's me. Your daughter," Amy confirmed for her. This only caused Trish to sob bitterly as she tugged on Amy's hand, pulling her down to her chest. Amy's hands went around her mother, and without warning, she too started to sob uncontrollably.

"I'm so-so sorry," Trish whispered against her hair, her voice filled with pain and regret.

"I know," Amy responded, not moving out of her mother's embrace.

"I love you so much," Trish spoke with much feeling. Amy didn't respond to her mother's declaration this time, and slowly, they separated.

Nikki stood watching their interaction with a satisfied grin on her face. She finally had her sister back in her life, and although it looked to be a long road to recovery, based on what Dr. Smith had told her, she was just happy Trish was still here in the land of the living. They had so much lost time to make up for. She had so much that she had to make up for. She also knew that both she and Trish had a lot of making up to do with Amy. This time, however, she was prepared to fight for the family she'd always wanted.

"I'm going to culinary school this fall, and I've already decided to stay here. So you just need to get better so we can work on our relationship," Amy was saying, scratching her arm nervously.

Trish nodded her head with a smile on her lips. Amy returned her smile, and Trish reached up to run her hand over her cheek. Amy reached up and placed her hand over Trish's, keeping it in place against her cheek.

Nikki smiled happily before her mind strayed. It amazed her how much accidents had the capability to repair broken families. Although she wasn't happy that the accident happened in the first place, it did far more than she had been willing to do to mend her relationship with Trish over the years.

Perhaps the accident had been a blessing in disguise.

Chapter Twenty-Seven

"**R**emember, only two people can visit with her at any time, and please make the visits shorter. It's almost time for her to get some rest," Dr. Smith advised the room full of persons who had come to visit Trish. Nikki nodded her head in agreement with what the doctor had just said. She'd left Amy in the room holding her mother's arm almost as if she were afraid to let go—as if she would disappear if she did.

Nikki re-entered the room with the first two visitors. She noticed that Amy was staring lovingly down at her mother whose eyes were also on her. They darted toward the door when it opened, and she smiled widely at the visitors.

"Paul," she said, beckoning to him.

"Hey, Trish," he greeted her with a broad grin. "It's good to see that you're still as tough as nails," he joked. Nikki chuckled softly.

"It's good to see your jokes are still as corny as I remember." Trish laughed, but it quickly turned into coughing that jolted her body with its force. Amy quickly reached for the cup of water and placed it at her mother's lips, urging her to take a drink.

When she finally calmed down, she turned back to Paul, who gave her an apologetic smile. "I'll hold the jokes until you're much better," he expressed.

Trish gave him an apologetic smile before her face dissolved into seriousness. "Thank you," she said, directing his gaze toward Amy. "Thank you for not giving up." She looked toward Amy lovingly.

"It was nothing. I'm just glad I could help." He played it off.

"Still, thank you," Trish repeated.

"There's someone else here to see you," Paul said, stepping aside so that she could see clearly who had been standing behind him.

Trish's eyes widened in surprise. "Reed," she said, a coy smile gracing her lips.

Paul looked over at Nikki, who inclined her head with a knowing grin. He excused himself and exited the room.

"Hi, Trish," Reed responded, smiling at her. "I'm happy to see that you're doing much better," he said, drawing closer to the bed.

"I'm glad you came," she responded, then averted her gaze to look at her hands.

Amy rose from the chair and walked over to where Nikki stood, watching their interaction.

"I've missed you. I mean, we've all missed you at the society," Reed said, staring at her while she continued to stare at her hands.

"Am I missing something?" Amy whispered to Nikki before looking back over at her mother and Reed. Nikki looked over at Amy before staring back at the two people across the room seemingly lost in their own little bubble.

"What do you think?" Nikki asked her.

Amy stared at them for a long while before turning back to Nikki. "I think they like each other," she assessed.

Nikki smiled over at her niece. "I think so too."

After Reed left, a few more of Trish's close friends and colleagues came to visit, including Kaylyn and Ryan.

In the end, only Nikki and Amy remained in the room with Trish, but a short while after, the doctor popped in to tell them that it was time for Trish to get some sleep. The two reluctantly left the room but promised to return first thing in the morning.

"Miss Murphy, may I have a word with you," the doctor requested when she was about to board the elevator.

"Sure thing," she agreed, before turning to Amy, who was already in the elevator with Paul. "I'll meet you guys downstairs," she said. They nodded before the doors closed, blocking them.

"I know you're all excited that Trish is finally awake, but like I said before, she has a long road to recovery, and the support from her family and friends will play an integral role in that recovery."

Nikki nodded her head in understanding.

"Trish has a broken leg. It'll take a little longer to heal than most breaks because of where the breaks are and their size. She also has head trauma, so we'll have to monitor her over the coming weeks to determine that there really aren't any adverse effects. She'll need a lot of physiotherapy to relearn how to use her limbs, and she'll also need counseling to cope with the trauma from the accident." After a short pause, the doctor turned serious eyes on her. "What I am telling you, Ms. Murphy, is that you have to be strong for her because there will be moments when she'll feel so weak that she wants to give up, and she may even lash out."

"I'm willing to do whatever it takes to make sure my sister gets better, Doctor," Nikki assured him with a look of determination.

"That's what I want to hear." Dr. Smith smiled.

The two parted, and Nikki made her way downstairs to find Paul and Amy by the car.

"Where's Reed?" she asked.

"He left. He said to tell you not to worry about the cleanup. They've got it under control," Paul informed her.

"What did the doctor say?" Amy asked expectantly.

"He was saying that we need to be there to help Trish in her recovery," she summarized.

Both Amy and Paul nodded in understanding. The three climbed into the car, and this time, Nikki sat up front.

As Paul cruised down Main Street, Nikki turned her body in the seat to look back at Amy. "I'm really proud of you, Amy, for how far you've come. I look at you, and all I see is a strong and determined young woman. You've faced so much more than a lot of us have, yet you still stand with your head held high. I can't wait to see what you do because I know it will be great." She smiled proudly at the young woman whose eyes shone with tears.

"Your aunt is right, Amy. You are a remarkable young woman, and I see a very bright future for you," Paul corroborated, looking at her through the rearview mirror.

"Thank you both. I appreciate it and am glad I have you both and Mom in my corner," Amy responded, smiling.

Nikki reached back to take her niece's hand and squeezed it lovingly.

After Paul dropped them off, Amy and Nikki headed straight for the kitchen. "You hungry?" Nikki asked as she reached up into the cupboard to remove a mug.

"I could eat," Amy replied.

Nikki recalled that they hadn't been able to eat anything from the fundraiser because of the call they'd received.

Walking over to the refrigerator, she removed the chicken lasagna she'd made the evening before. She eased a good portion of it onto two plates before warming them in the microwave. She then put a tea bag in the mug while she waited for the water in the kettle to boil. When the tea and food were ready, she placed Amy's before her on the island and took a seat across from her. They both dug into the meal almost immediately.

"So..."

Amy looked up from taking another bite of the lasagna to look at Nikki.

She put down her cup to give her niece her undivided attention. "How do you feel about today?" she asked.

Amy's brows furrowed in thought as her eyes took on a faraway look. Finally, her eyes focused back on Nikki as she replied. "I feel happy, relieved, but also fearful."

Nikki's chin jerked downward before coming back up in understanding.

"I'm glad my mom is awake. The feelings that I have toward her are kind of new to me because I've always wanted a mother who would love me and want me as much as I wanted her, but with my adoptive mother, I always wondered if she even liked me, especially after she started acting cold toward me after I called the police on her husband."

Nikki's heart constricted from the pain she felt oozing

out of Amy as she spoke, and she wished there was some way she could erase all those bad memories and replace them with good ones.

"I have a lot of questions that I want to ask her, but I'm afraid that it'll make her treat me differently." Her eyes flicked downward in guilt.

Nikki reached over to rest her hand over the one Amy rested on the island. Amy looked up at her, her eyes filled with pain.

"Trish isn't like that, Amy. She was prepared to look for you because she wants you with all her heart. I know she has prepared for your questions, and nothing could make her want you less. If anything, she's afraid of you not wanting her and her losing you again."

A tear slipped and fell down Amy's cheek, and Nikki reached over to wipe it away. "Your mother...Trish loves you very much, and I need you to understand that you have a right to ask the tough questions without fear of rejection."

"I wish she hadn't given me up," Amy said timidly.

Nikki brushed the back of her hand against Amy's cheek. "I know," she spoke solemnly. "For now, let's just try to live in the now and face the challenges and the questions as they come together, okay?"

Amy nodded her head as she agreed, "Okay."

Just then, Amy's cell rang. She fished it out of her pocket to see who it was. Her eyes widened in surprise, then they flickered to Nikki, who stared back at her in concern.

"What is it?" she asked.

"It's the detective assigned to the case," she informed her before lifting the phone to her ear. "Hello?"

Nikki watched her niece as she gave clipped answers

to whatever the detective was saying to her. When she finally ended the call, Nikki was on edge as she watched Amy's face go pale.

"Amy. Was it about Jake?" she asked.

Amy looked up, her mouth opening and closing like a fish out of water. "Jake is back in jail," she finally managed to say.

"Really?" Nikki asked, surprised. "Why?"

"He was booked in Seattle for assault and battery. He badly beat another girl, and she ended up in the hospital."

"Oh no. That's horrible," Nikki exclaimed in alarm.

Amy nodded; her lips pursed together in a thin line. "The detective says with my case, this one, and his priors, he's looking to go away for a long time."

"Good riddance," Nikki said with disdain. "How are you feeling?"

"Honestly, I'm relieved that he's in jail, but I'm also saddened by the fact that another woman had to suffer such abuse for him to finally get what he deserves."

"It is sad," Nikki agreed. "But sometimes we have to celebrate the wins and look on the bright side. He won't be able to hurt anyone else for a long time," she reasoned.

Amy nodded. She sighed deeply and turned to Nikki with disappointment etched in her brows. "I can't believe I was such a fool to trust him and believe that he could change because he claimed to love me."

"None of this is your fault, Amy," Nikki rushed in to say. "You were fooled by what he presented because he was a sick and manipulative person preying on your insecurities. That doesn't make it your fault because if you had known the kind of person he was from the beginning, you would never have gotten involved with him."

Amy gave her aunt a small smile of appreciation. "I'm just sorry I gave him so much of me." She sighed.

"I know, sweetheart. I know." Nikki rounded the island and pulled Amy into her arms, offering the comfort she knew she needed. "With time, the betrayal and hurt will go away, and you will be able to open your heart to someone who truly deserves your love. Someone who will cherish you for the gem you are," Nikki assured her.

"Come on, let's go," Nikki instructed when they separated.

"Where are we going?" Amy asked with furrowed brows.

"We're going for a walk on the beach to clear our minds," Nikki replied, holding out her hand to Amy. A broad smile transformed Amy's face as she hooked her hand in the crook of Nikki's arm.

The two exited the house and made their way across the lawn, into the grove of evergreens at the back of the property, and finally down the uneven terrain toward the distant sound of crashing waves.

Chapter Twenty-Eight

P aul finished adding the whipped cream to the cheesecake just as the timer went off. Putting on a pair of mittens, he headed for the stove.

"All right, hold your horses. I'm here," he said, opening the oven to stop the incessant buzzing. Reaching into the scalding heat, he removed the pan with the roasted pork. Using a carving knife, he cut into the meat, and a wide grin was plastered on his face at how easily the blade sliced through it and how pink it was on the inside as the juices oozed from the succulent flesh.

"Look at this beauty," he marveled, satisfied with his work. He put the pan back into the welcoming warmth of the oven and turned his attention to the boiled potatoes. He stripped them from their skin before placing them in a bowl and mashing and grating cheddar cheese over them, then whisking them until they made the perfect, fluffy, creamy cloud. Setting that aside, he removed the cherry farro salad from the refrigerator, topping it up with some sweet vinaigrette he'd made from scratch.

As Paul was adding the finishing touches, the doorbell

rang. He removed his apron, hung it on the hook behind the kitchen door, and made his way to the front door. A huge grin split his face as he opened the door.

"Hi, Dad," Sarah greeted, just before he swept her into his arms for a bear hug, lifting her off the ground. Sarah laughed in glee.

"Hi, sweetie," he returned.

After placing her back on her feet, he turned to Aaron and gave him a milder version of the hug he did with his daughter. "Aaron, it's good to see you both. What's it been five years since we had a get-together like this?"

"Ha ha. Very funny, Dad. I know we're long overdue a visit, but you don't have to be so dramatic," Sarah chimed in, walking through the door with Aaron following her closely. "By the way, it smells like heaven in here," she said, releasing a satisfied groan.

"I can't wait to taste everything," she threw over her shoulder.

"Just like old times," Paul said jokingly, closing the front door and following them into the dining room.

"Wow, Dad, you really outdid yourself. Everything looks absolutely scrumptious," Sarah complimented, staring down at the spread on the table.

"It really does," Aaron agreed.

Paul smiled, full of pride. "Wait until you taste it," he said promisingly.

After they all sat around the table and Aaron said grace, they eagerly dug into the food, making sounds of approval.

"Wine?" he offered. Aaron held out his glass, allowing Paul to pour the rich red liquid into it.

"Not for me," Sarah declined. "I'll just have some water."

"How is work?" he asked.

"Busy," Sarah and Aaron both said at the same time. They looked over at each other and smiled.

"It's been a hectic couple of months, and with us being nurses and our schedules, we sometimes find it difficult to be in the same place for more than just a few minutes, but we're trying to make it work so that we'll have more time together," Aaron explained.

"That's the best place to start when trying to make your relationship work. You have to find time to spend with each other, and by that, I mean quality time; find a middle ground," Paul advised, taking a sip of his wine.

Aaron and Sarah exchanged a look he couldn't quite decipher. He wondered what it was about.

"You're about to get married, and that changes everything. Compromises have to be made. You have to be prepared for anything and realize that marriage, like every other relationship, takes work. It takes you two choosing to be in it for the long haul and doing everything it takes to hold the framework together. When you start having children, you'll understand it even more."

"Well...it's a little too late for that now," Sarah responded.

Paul looked over at his daughter quizzically before turning questioning eyes to his son-in-law.

"We were going to wait until after the meal to tell you, but..."

Paul's brows scrunched together in confusion as he watched his daughter reach down into her bag before coming up with a few items that she proceeded to lay out on the table before him. His eyes widened in realization.

"Congratulations, Grandpa."

Paul looked from the onesie and baby socks to his daughter's smiling face.

"You're pregnant?" he asked softly.

Sarah nodded her head in confirmation.

The chair tipped back, almost falling with how quickly Paul got out of it and went to his daughter, pulling her from her own chair and wrapping her up in his arms.

"I'm going to be a grandpa," he said with emotion. He turned to Aaron, pulling him up for a hug.

"My baby is going to have a baby, and I'm about to be a grandfather," he repeated in awe. Sarah laughed at how stunned he was.

"I can't wait to tell Nikki that I'm about to be a grandad." His eyes widened in realization. "I mean—"

"Relax, Dad. I know what you mean." Sarah smirked.

"This calls for a special treat," he said, changing the line of conversation. "Good thing I chose to make your favorite."

"What?" Sarah asked, her eyes glittering with enthusiasm.

"Strawberry cheesecake."

"Yay!" his daughter exclaimed, throwing her arms up in the air.

Paul laughed as he went into the kitchen and removed the sweet confection from the refrigerator. Cutting a reasonable slice for each of them, he brought back the cake to the dining room. Sarah immediately tucked into hers, earning a few chuckles from Paul and Aaron. Aaron took a few bites of his own piece, then without warning, his pager went off. He reached down to look at it, and his face fell.

"It's work," he informed the table. "I gotta go."

"That's fine, babe. I understand," Sarah assured him.

"I'll take Sarah home when we're done here," Paul informed him.

"Okay, see you later," he said, placing a quick kiss against Sarah's lips and turning to leave. "Thanks for dinner, Paul. I really appreciate it."

"Don't mention it," Paul responded. Aaron gave him a grateful smile before heading for the door.

When they finished eating their cake, Paul suggested they sit out on the back porch, which Sarah agreed to. They made their way outside and settled into the Adirondacks facing the water. The two sat in comfortable silence, taking in the soft orange and pink hues of twilight as the ebb and flow of the ocean filled the air in a tranquil manner. Even the chirping of crickets out in the shrubs added to the light ambience.

"I miss this," Sarah said, causing Paul to turn his head to look over at her. "We haven't done this in a long while. I'm grateful for it."

Paul's gaze returned to the water as he nodded in understanding. "Are you happy, Sarah?" he asked.

His daughter looked over at him, and he turned to look back at her. "I am happy, Dad," she replied with a bright smile. "I haven't been this happy since..."

"Since your mother," Paul finished for her.

Sarah nodded. "Ever since she died, it's felt as if she took a piece of me with her. But now, with this pregnancy and the fact that I am marrying the man I love very much, it feels like I've healed," she offered.

"I'm glad for that," Paul responded. "I only want you to be happy, and no matter what that entails, I want you to know that I'll always be here for you," he said seriously.

Sarah smiled appreciatively back at him before

turning her head forward, but just as quickly, it jerked back in his direction, and a smirk played on her lips.

"Now that we've spoken about my personal life, it's time to delve into yours," she said.

Paul pulled himself up in the chair as he prepared himself for her question.

"Have you ever thought about getting back in the saddle? What about going on a date?"

Paul gave a short laugh as he considered her question. He drew in a deep breath before releasing it and turning back to her.

"I have thought about it. Dating, I mean."

"But?" Sarah pressed.

Paul released another heavy breath, and his head swiveled back around to stare ahead of him once more.

"I am hesitant to put myself out there because it feels like a betrayal to Nat and what we shared," he confessed.

Sarah bobbed her head contemplatively.

"I also don't want to damage our relationship by adding someone new to the dynamics." He looked over at her.

Sarah's brow furrowed in confusion.

"You've only ever witnessed your mother and me together, and in that lifetime, we were very happy and in love. I'm afraid that if I find that with someone else, it will hurt you, and I wouldn't forgive myself if I ever became the cause of your pain," he revealed.

"Dad, I'm not fourteen anymore," she spoke seriously. "I will always remember the love that you shared with Mom because those are memories I cherish and carry with me, but I won't hold it against you if you choose to find love again because you deserve it. I know Mom would have wanted you to be happy too. You can't shut yourself off from being truly happy just because you're scared it'll hurt me. Your happiness is solely yours and no one else's."

Paul stretched over to push back a curl from her face affectionately. "When did you get so wise?" he asked in awe.

Sarah laughed. "Life has a way of teaching you a lot of lessons that you never thought you'd need. From a rebellious teenager to this, I can't say I'm disappointed."

"Neither am I," Paul said proudly.

Sarah smiled affectionately back at him after, and the two settled into a comfortable silence for a few minutes.

"After your heart attack, I was so scared that I had lost you. But then it occurred to me that I ran the chance of still losing you if you didn't get to live the rest of your life in a fulfilling way. I realized that you could possibly find love again. When I saw how much you cared for Nikki, there was no way I could deny you that."

Sarah looked over at him, her eyes brimming with affection. "You look at her the way you used to look at Mom, and that's not a bad thing. I've also witnessed how easy it is for you to do anything for her without hesitation or question, and before you say that's how you are with everyone, I've seen you interact with others. This is way different, and you know it."

Paul closed his mouth, unable to refute her statement.

"I'm pretty sure she has feelings for you too so that makes it even better. And I like her too, so that's a big plus."

Paul chuckled at this, and Sarah joined in with him.

The LED bulbs came on, brightening the porch and making it easier for Paul to see his daughter's face as the sky darkened even further.

Sarah gave him a serious look. "You need to tell her how you feel," she advised.

Paul smiled at his daughter, his eyes twinkling in admiration.

"Come here," he instructed. Sarah left her own chair and went to curl up against her father as he held her, and they looked out at the first set of stars peppering the darkened sky.

"I love you, sweetie."

"I love you too, Dad," Sarah responded.

Paul smiled as his thoughts switched to Nikki. He had a lot to think about and some decisions to make.

Chapter Twenty-Nine

"Knock, knock," Nikki said as she entered her sister's room with a wide grin on her lips.

"Hey." Trish smiled as she sat up in bed.

"Hey," Nikki returned. "How was therapy?" she asked, setting down the bag of personal items she'd brought on the table.

Trish didn't reply.

It had been two weeks since Trish opened her eyes, and she'd only started therapy four days ago. She could tell she was frustrated by the progress, but it was to be expected. Plus, the doctor had already prepped them on what to expect.

Nikki turned to stare at her expectantly.

"How is Amy?" Trish asked, attempting to change the subject.

"Amy's fine. She's over at Lot 28," Nikki answered. "Now, back to your therapy. How was it?"

Trish released a heavy sigh. "Tedious," she responded, looking away from Nikki.

"It'll get better. Just hang in there. You're making

great progress," Nikki said with an encouraging smile. "I brought you something, but I had to sneak it past the nurses," she said, pulling a Hershey bar from her pocket. Trish's eyes lit up as a bright smile lifted her lips.

"I remember this was your favorite candy back when we were kids."

"It still is," Trish replied, holding her hand out for the chocolate.

Nikki laughed at how eager she was. She placed it in her hands and watched her with a tender smile as she removed the top of the wrapper and took a bite of the chocolate bar. Her moan of satisfaction caused Nikki to chortle.

"I remembered how you would take all of your money to buy these Snickers bars and how I had to vouch for you every time with Dad for buying it even though he forbade you."

Trish released a laugh of her own. "I remember."

"Those were some great times," Nikki reminisced. A melancholic smile graced her lips as she looked out the window at the moving objects. "We were happy and had more freedom to be children."

She turned to see Trish looking at her with remorse in her eyes. "Having parents who only required perfection really did a number on us, huh?" She sighed dejectedly.

Nikki walked over to sit on the bed.

"I'm sorry I didn't give Amy to you, Nikki. I should have trusted you," Trish spoke, her eyes clouded by regret. "My greatest regret has been giving up my daughter." Her voice broke at the end as she struggled to keep in her tears.

"Trish, losing Amy was not your fault," Nikki spoke with assurance. "Our parents are the real culprits here. I understand now that you had no choice. What you did took courage, and I want you to know I am proud of you."

"I don't think Amy will see it that way," Trish said, tucking her chin into her chest.

"Trish, Amy understands that your choices weren't as varied back then. All you have to do now is be honest with her. I promise you, she'll understand."

Trish nodded her head in understanding. Nikki reached over and held her sister's hand. Trish turned to look at her.

"I'm very proud of the woman you are today, Trish. What happened to you back then could have broken you, but it didn't. You took control of your life, and you made something great. Those are the same qualities I see in Amy. She is not easily broken. She is a determined young woman, and I'm beginning to witness that she has a very caring heart, just like you."

Trish's face lit up at this. "I still can't believe she's actually here, on Camano Island," she marveled.

"All because of your own efforts," Nikki reminded her with a smile.

Trish returned her smile. "I love her so much already, and it keeps growing every time I see her. It's so much that it feels like my chest would burst open."

"I know what you mean," Nikki agreed.

Trish's eyes took on a faraway look as she said, "I remember when the doctor first placed her in my arms. I was overwhelmed with love for this little human life that I had made." She turned hopeful eyes to Nikki. "I can't wait to shower her with all the love she deserves."

Nikki smiled knowingly.

"Speaking of love, when are you going to finally admit

that you have feelings for Paul?" Trish asked, staring directly into her sister's eyes.

Nikki's eyes widened in surprise as she sputtered to speak, "Wha-what are you talking about?"

"I'm talking about how his eyes follow you whenever you're not looking, and I witnessed you do it to him too. I picked up on it from the first day you both came here."

"Trish," she cautioned. "I don't think it is a good idea to entertain those thoughts, especially with everything going on."

"You're making excuses," Trish deadpanned.

Nikki felt warmth cover her hand resting on top of the bed, and she looked back at Trish staring at her in understanding.

"I know you might be feeling a bit scared, but you deserve to be happy, and I can remember from back when you were in high school that Paul was the only person who made you happy. It's time to give yourself the chance to be happy again."

"I'll think about it," Nikki promised with a reassuring smile.

* * *

"Nelly, it's so good to see you," Nikki greeted the gray-eyed, silver-haired woman sitting by a table close to the door in Lot 28.

"It is nice to see you too, my dear. How is your sister?"

"She's much better. She improves daily."

"That's great news. It's good to know my prayers were answered. Thank you, Lord," Nelly praised, looking at the sky.

Nikki gave a small chuckle at the woman's flamboyant

gesture. "Thank you for what you're doing, Nelly, and please don't stop doing it," she encouraged.

"I will keep praying, then," Nelly said.

Nikki reached over and grasped the older woman's hand.

"I know you don't mind keeping a poor old soul like me company, but I think someone needs it more than I do," Nelly said, looking behind Nikki.

Nikki turned in the direction the old woman's chin jutted toward, and her heart slammed against her chest when she saw Paul standing there staring back at her. He walked toward her, and Nikki felt as if her heart would beat out of her chest.

"Good afternoon, ladies," he greeted when he stopped at the table.

"Good afternoon, young man. Have you come to steal my companion away?" Nelly asked, narrowing her eyes in a way to make her look menacing.

Paul released a small chuckle. "Only to borrow her, Miss Nelly." He looked over at Nikki, a smile teasing his lips.

"Of course. You have my blessing," Nelly released.

"Wait, I'm right here, and I didn't agree to this," Nikki sputtered in mock annoyance.

"Oh hush, child, and just go," Nelly waved her toward Paul.

"Thanks, Miss Nelly. I owe you one," Paul said gratefully, indicating for Nikki to follow him toward the patio area. Nikki turned to give Nelly a *why'd you do that* look. The woman stared blankly back at her before the sign of a smirk lifted her lips just as Nikki turned.

Paul led her across the patio and along the path toward the sandy beach coast in the distance. The two kept pace with each other, but neither exchanged a word, both caught up in their own thoughts. When they made it to the beachfront, Nikki allowed the sand to run over her sandals and through her toes as they walked along the grainy path. They came to a stop at some distance down the beach and turned to look out at the blue waters reflecting the cloudless sky.

"You know, the last time we were on the beach like this, we were a couple, and I had a very important question I wanted to ask you," Paul spoke, breaking the silence.

Nikki turned to stare questioningly up at him.

"I had a speech, the ring, and reservations for a restaurant back in Seattle for us."

Nikki's eyes widened in surprise, and her hands went to her lips, covering them.

"I was prepared to propose to you, Nikki," he said seriously.

His confession caught her off guard, and her heart continued to hammer against her chest as all thoughts flew out of her head.

"But then you said we needed to break up, and like a fool, I agreed instead of fighting for you and for what we had." He chuckled, the sound void of mirth.

"I loved you, but it wasn't enough."

"That's not true, Paul. It was enough," she refuted, finding her voice. "Maybe if you had asked me before my parents manipulated me the way they did, we would be different people walking on this beach right now."

She turned and looked up at Paul, her eyes filled with regret. "Those words that I spoke that day, they weren't mine. They were from my parents," she revealed. "They drilled it into me, convincing me it was for the best. I cried for a whole week after our breakup. That's how much I loved you, but then I had to do what my parents expected of me, so I locked away my feelings and pushed on, trying to forget you and all that we'd shared." Nikki sighed dejectedly. "I have so many regrets," she breathed out before looking up at Paul, her eyes full of sorrow.

"It's okay. I've come to accept that it wasn't our time," Paul assured her. "Things played out exactly as they should have, and from it, I learned to love again, and I got a beautiful daughter in the process." He smiled.

Nikki returned the smile.

"But now, the cards are squaring up right to this moment, and I am not letting the opportunity slip through my fingers again." Paul turned to fully face Nikki, his eyes bright and determined.

"I love you, Nikki. I have always loved you, even in the times that we were apart, and although I am grateful for the life I lived with Natalie, to deny the fact that you've always been there in my heart would be to deny my happiness, and I am tired of doing that."

Her heart skipped a beat, and the butterflies that had taken up permanent residence in her stomach skittered as they cascaded over each other. Her mouth opened, but no words came out.

"Say something, please," Paul begged her.

As hard as she tried to say something, her tongue seemed fixed to the roof of her mouth, making it difficult for her to talk.

Paul's face fell at her lack of response, and without a word, he turned to make his way back up the beach.

Her heart beat rapidly and a ringing sound in her ears as she panicked that she was about to blow another shot at happiness.

"Wait," she managed to force through her lips. She couldn't allow him to leave without her being able to voice how she really felt about him. How she'd always felt about him.

Paul stopped in his tracks and turned to face her once more, his eyes guarded.

Still, no words came from her lips, and when he made to turn and continue walking, she marched up to him and pulled his head down to hers. Their lips met in a slow, endearing kiss. At that moment, she was sure he could feel all of the love she had for him.

When they finally separated, her words rushed out unbridled. "I love you, Paul. I've never stopped loving you, and I don't think I ever could, even if I wanted to."

A broad smile made its way onto Paul's face, and he drew her in for another sweet kiss.

"What took you so long?" he asked when they separated again.

Nikki gave him a sheepish smile.

"I'm sorry that it always takes a little more time for me to tell you how I truly feel," she apologized. "I want you to know that this time I'm all in," she promised.

Paul smiled lovingly down at her before fixing his lips against hers once more and lifting her into his arms.

Epilogue

"Nikki, we gotta go now. We're already a half hour late," Paul's voice rang out with impatience. He glanced down at his watch, his brows furrowing before he looked up at her.

"Just...a few...more...There. I'm done," she said triumphantly before carefully making her way down the ladder. Paul held it in place until she stepped off the last rung.

"Thank you for keeping me steady." She smiled innocently up at his scowling face.

"You're a riot, do you know that?" Paul chuckled, unable to remain mad when she was smiling at him like she was.

Nikki's smile grew even wider, and she leaned forward and pecked his chin before stepping back. "That's why you love me." She smirked.

Paul groaned. "I don't remember you being this mischievous."

"That's because there are a lot more layers to me than

back when we were in high school," she expressed. "What are you doing?" Nikki asked, pulling back in alarm when Paul lightly scraped his finger up her arm.

"Looking for your layers," he replied in an isn't it obvious voice. He burst into laughter when she huffed, and her arms banded across her chest.

"You, Paul Thompson, are not funny," Nikki pouted with a roll of her eyes, then turned her back to him.

A kiss landed on her cheek that sent instant warmth to them. She turned around to face the man smiling affectionately back at her. "That's why we're perfect for each other," he stated. Instantly, Nikki's frown dissolved, and her lips turned up at the corners.

"Anyway, what do you think?" She jutted her chin upward at the banner she'd spent the past half hour hanging up.

Paul looked up at her handiwork and nodded in approval. "It looks great, but we really gotta go. I'm sure Trish is probably wondering where we are by now, and she might get suspicious and start having ideas."

"You're right. We need to go. Just let me get Amy and leave some instructions with Kaylyn, and then we can leave."

"All right. I'll put this away and meet you two by the car," Paul responded, lifting the ladder and heading toward the front door.

Nikki turned in the opposite direction, making her way toward the back porch where she could already hear the chatter from the guests they'd invited over for Trish's welcome home party. She greeted by a flurry of activity the moment she threw the back door open and stepped onto the porch.

The sweet, smoky scent of barbecued ribs wafted to her nostrils, and her eyes instantly found Reed at the grill, turning slabs of meat as the rising smoke and heat fused with them to create an authentic, salivating aroma.

She definitely wanted a rack of those ribs when she got back from the hospital.

"Nikki, I thought you'd be gone by now," Kaylyn said as she sidled up to her.

"I'm leaving now. I just need to find Amy," she replied, looking around in hopes of spotting her niece.

"Oh, I saw Amy heading over to the Nestled Inn with your friend Ava," Kaylyn informed her.

"Thanks," Nikki replied, turning around to leave. "I'll text you when we've got Trish. Make sure everyone moves to the living room and is quiet until I give you the signal," she instructed.

"Will do," Kaylyn replied with a thumbs-up.

Nikki made her way to the front and found Paul leaning against the driver's side of his car with his arms folded against his chest.

Nikki gave him an apologetic look.

"Where's Amy?" he asked, looking behind her.

"She's by the inn. I'll go get her."

"I thought that's what you were doing in the first place," Paul said, easing into his car and starting the engine, then honking his horn.

Amy came running down the porch steps before Nikki had taken more than ten steps.

"Sorry." She smiled sheepishly at her aunt.

"It's okay, but we're very late. Your mother must be worrying by now."

The women got into the car, and Paul drove off the property and onto the main road. In less than twenty minutes, they were riding the elevator up to the fourth floor where Trish was.

"Sorry."

"Sorry," Nikki and Amy apologized for their lateness as they hustled past the two nurses standing by their station whose unsmiling gazes had landed on them the moment they came through the elevator.

"We're not the ones you should be worried about," one of the women responded with a smirk.

Nikki pushed the door open and entered the room to find her sister sitting on the bed, her cell phone in her hand. Trish's eyes registered surprise when they landed on Nikki before they narrowed.

"I was just about to send out a search party for you," she said lightly, but the slight wobble in her voice told Nikki that her lateness had affected her. She felt awful.

"I'm sorry, Trish. I should have been here a lot sooner," Nikki apologized.

Trish gave her half a smile. "That's okay," she responded softly.

Nikki knew it wasn't. Ever since Trish had woken up over a month ago, she'd had to work very hard to regain functionality in her limbs, which had almost become flaccid as her muscles were wasted from lack of use. She'd had to relearn how to walk again, and her broken leg had healed, but she still hadn't fully recovered and had to use a cane for support. She'd done one reconstructive facial surgery, and her bandages were now all gone, but there were a few noticeable scars on her forehead. Her physiotherapist had said her improvements were all on track. Still, even though that was good news, Nikki realized that her sister struggled to cope with the emotional trauma from the accident and her recovery.

Sometimes she felt so helpless, especially when Trish got into a pensive mood like now, as she stared down at her feet.

"I have a surprise for you," she said, causing Trish's head to lift to stare at her curiously.

Nikki walked over to the door and opened it, revealing Amy.

"Hi, Mom," Amy greeted with a wide grin as she walked into the room.

"Hi, sweetie. What are you doing here? Don't you have classes today?" Trish asked, furrowing her brows. However, this time, a small smile graced her lips.

"I do. I did. But I decided to take the day to help Aunt Nikki get you back home, where you belong," Amy replied, reaching for the hand her mother held out to her and holding it against her chest, an endearing smile on her lips.

Trish's smile brightened as she stared lovingly back at her daughter. "I'm glad you came," she said in earnest.

"Me too," Amy replied.

"What did I miss?" Paul asked, stepping into the room with a blank expression.

The woman chuckled, and Amy released her mother's hand but remained close to her.

"Hey, Paul," Trish greeted him with a smile.

Paul smiled back. "You look in high spirits," he observed.

"I am now," Trish replied, reaching for Amy's hand and squeezing it lovingly.

"That's great news. Are you guys ready to go?"

The women nodded before filing out of the room and heading for the elevator. They waved goodbye to the smiling nurses just before the elevator dinged shut, and they zoomed to the main lobby. Nikki held the door open for Trish and Paul, who assisted her through it.

Trish sat in the back with Amy while Nikki rode up front with Paul. As the vehicle moved along the road, Nikki searched out Trish in the rearview mirror, but Trish was smiling over at Amy. This brought a smile to Nikki's face. She took out her phone and quickly shot a message to Kaylyn. Almost instantly, her phone pinged in response. Bringing up her messages, she noticed the woman sent her a thumbs-up emoji.

When they finally made it back to the house, Paul helped Trish get out of the car. She exchanged a knowing look with Amy as they ascended the porch steps ahead of them. Nikki rattled the doorknob as she tried to open the door.

"Oh, I forgot, I didn't use the key," she said loudly, slapping her hand against her forehead. "Let me just..." She rummaged through her purse before finally lifting the key above her head and jingling it in triumph. "Here it is. Now I can open the door."

Trish's brows launched upward as she stared at her sister in confusion.

Nikki finally opened the door after three attempts as Trish stared questioningly at her. She moved aside, allowing Paul and Trish to go ahead. Just as they approached the wall that opened into the living room, Nikki said. "I was thinking maybe we could go out to eat, or if you're not up to it, we could get a table at Lot 28!"

Trish looked weirdly at her sister. "Why do you keep do—"

"SURPRISE!"

Trish jumped back, and her hands clutched her chest as her eyes widened with surprise at the mass of smiling faces. Without warning, she burst into tears, effectively wiping the smiles off their faces as they stared at a sobbing Trish in concern.

"You guys"—*Sniff*—"I can't believe you did this for"—*Sniff*—"Me." Her eyes lifted above their heads to stare appreciatively at the welcome home sign attached to the curtain.

"Wait until you see what's on the outside," someone called out, earning chuckles from the group.

"Still, thank you guys so much for this," she said in earnest as a few more tears rolled down her cheeks.

"You deserve it, Trish, and so much more. We are just happy that you found your way back to us," Kaylyn responded, walking over and pulling her into a tight hug.

Nikki smiled affectionately at her friend and worker the minute they separated.

Just like that, Trish accepted the hugs and encouragement from the townspeople while thanking them for their support.

"Hi, Trish," Reed greeted her with a warm, affectionate smile.

"Reed," Trish responded with a coy smile.

"You look...lovely," he complimented.

Nikki noticed the way her sister's cheeks became rosy as a sweet smile turned her lips upward. She exchanged knowing looks with Paul and inclined her head in nonverbal agreement to give them some privacy.

"All right, everyone, let's make our way outside. That's where the real party is after all. Let's give Trish a little time to breathe and regroup before she joins us," Nikki instructed. The crowd dispersed quickly, leaving Reed and Trish staring shyly back at each other.

Nikki and Paul exited the house and joined in the

festivities. She eagerly tucked into the succulent rack of ribs she'd been craving, and she moaned in satisfaction that it did not disappoint.

A little while later, Trish exited the house using Reed's arm for support instead of her cane. Again, the crowd erupted in cheers for her, and her smile only grew wider as Reed escorted her down the steps, holding her protectively at his side.

"I brought you some punch. Thought you might be thirsty."

Nikki smiled over at Paul as she gladly took the drink and took some sips. Paul's arms came around her shoulders, pulling her against him in a sideways hug as he placed a kiss against her temple.

Nikki couldn't help the slight shiver that traveled up her spine at his show of affection. She didn't think she would ever get used to how good and natural it felt to be with him.

She felt his fingers along her chin, turning her head, and she eagerly complied, looking into his green eyes that stared back at her.

"Are you happy?" he asked. His eyes studied her closely as he waited for her to respond.

"I am happy," she finally responded with conviction, smiling up at him.

And she was.

She turned and stared appreciatively at the scene before her; at Trish being hugged and coddled by Kaylyn and the others, Reed hovering close by protectively, and Amy laughing at whatever Sarah, whose baby bump was very noticeable, said to her. Her eyes flickered to her best friend in deep conversation with Nelly, and she wondered if there would be a better scene than this.

Just then, she felt something soft rub up against her leg. She looked down to see Tabby staring up at her as she released a soft meow. She felt another pair of eyes on her, and she complied with the magnetic pull she felt, turning to look back at Paul as he stared lovingly back at her.

At that moment, she knew she had made the right decision, and she could not be happier.

Coming Next

Coming Next

Pre order Hearts Reawakened

Other Books by Kimberly

The Archer Inn

An Oak Harbor Series

A Yuletide Creek Series

A Festive Christmas Series

A Cape Cod Series

Connect with Kimberly Thomas

Amazon
Facebook
Newsletter
BookBub

To receive exclusive updates from Kimberly, please sign up to be on her Newsletter!

CLICK HERE TO SUBSCRIBE

Made in United States
North Haven, CT
05 February 2025

65415267R00141